IF WE WERE GIANTS

IF WE WERE GIANTS

A NOVEL BY DAVE MATTHEWS

WITH CLETE BARRETT SMITH

DISNEY • HYPERION

LOS ANGELES   NEW YORK

Copyright © 2020 by Disney Enterprises, Inc.
Illustrations by Antonio Javier Caparo

First Hardcover Edition, March 2020
First Paperback Edition, March 2021
1 3 5 7 9 10 8 6 4 2
FAC-025438-21015
Printed in the United States of America

This book is set in Adobe Garamond Pro/Fontspring
Designed by Marci Senders

Library of Congress Cataloging-in-Publication Control Number: 2018048430
ISBN 978-1-368-01869-2

Visit www.DisneyBooks.com

SUSTAINABLE
FORESTRY
INITIATIVE

Certified Sourcing

www.sfiprogram.org
SFI-01054

The SFI label applies to the text stock

Part One
The Volcano

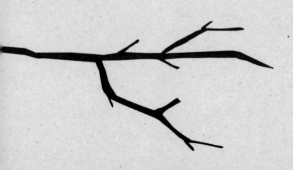

1

ONLY A FEW PEOPLE were ever allowed to venture past the borders of Zedu. Ten-year-old Kirra was one of them.

She should have been constantly aware that this was a great and serious responsibility. She should have remained on high alert for the many dangers. She should have made careful note of everything she saw and heard to bring knowledge back to her people.

But mostly she liked to chase squirrels.

Every square inch of the limited space back in Zedu was claimed for something useful—crop terraces, or thatched huts, or grazing plots for livestock. But here on the Outside, Kirra loved how the whole world could just relax and stretch itself right out. There were no forests inside the confines of Zedu's walls, and out here, the miles upon miles of tall trees made for an irresistible playground. Her small feet were perfect for racing along branches—even the narrow ones—and her light body allowed her to take flying leaps from one tree to another without breaking the limbs in her sure-handed grip as she swung from them.

And there were squirrels. So many squirrels. It was Kirra's goal to capture one and bring it home to show Tiko, mostly because he just shook his head when she described the cutest creature she had ever seen. As much as her little brother loved hearing her stories about the Outside, she could tell he didn't believe half of them.

The squirrel she was after made its big mistake after leading Kirra up a hundred feet. Had it kept climbing, she might have eventually given up. But the creature suddenly shifted and changed course, apparently thinking it would have a better chance of escape on the ground, and it started scrambling down the tree trunk.

Kirra, red-faced and panting after the long chase, suddenly had the advantage. Going down was much easier than climbing up. With a fearlessness that had always inspired envy in her brother and horror in her mother, Kirra hopped from branch to branch, scarcely balancing on one foot before bounding to the next limb, more like controlled falling than climbing down. So she was already on firm footing when the squirrel came blindly barreling down the tree trunk.

Kirra waited . . . waited . . . and then suddenly lunged. She came away with two handfuls of squirming fur.

"Aha! Finally got one!"

She wasn't sure who was more surprised—she or the squirrel. But as she watched it scrabble its tiny paws against her hands and frantically turn its head this way and that, she suddenly felt pity for it. After all, squirrels enjoyed running free through these glorious trees as much as she did.

Kirra tilted her head and studied the creature. "So what do you think I should do with you?"

The squirrel stopped squirming, looked right at her, and unleashed a stream of chittering.

"You sound like Maja when she's mad," Kirra said, smiling.

This observation didn't sit well with the creature. It started thrashing around even more in its frenzied attempt to escape. Kirra held it in a gentle yet firm grip, then carefully removed one hand from the squirrel and felt for the pouch tied to her waist. She had brought it especially to carry back a fine specimen such as this. . . .

But she just couldn't do it.

Kirra knelt on the forest floor. "You're lucky I have such a soft heart today, my furry friend." She lowered her hands to set it gently on the ground, but instead, the squirrel turned and, in a flash, raced up the length of her arm, scrambled onto the top of her head, and—digging its little paws into her thick hair—launched itself back into the tree, where it disappeared into the branches.

Kirra smirked and shook her head. She was brushing dirt and little wisps of fur off of her hands, when—

"Kirra!"

Uh-oh. Her father. And the sound of his voice was so faint, she must have traveled farther than she'd meant to.

"Kiiir-ra!"

Much farther. She could barely hear him. That was not good.

She ran in the direction of the voice, quickly finding the way blocked by thickets of brush, fallen logs, and rotting stumps with plants growing straight out of their tops.

Better to go up and over.

Kirra jumped to grab a low-hanging branch with both hands, pulled herself up, and swung her body around until she was straddling it. Then she hopped to her feet, ran along the sturdy limb, and leaped off, grabbing at the branches of the next tree. These were thinner and much more pliable, and she swung through the air in a dizzying rush, the broad leaves swiping her face, until she was able to pull herself hand over hand to thicker branches closer to the trunk.

Then she scaled the limbs, ten, twenty, feet off the ground, and jumped to the next tree.

"Kir-ra!"

Closer now. She angled over to her left, bounced across a half-dozen more trees, and could finally see the trunks thinning out where the wide dirt road snaked through the forest.

Soon she was able to get a glimpse of Taro. Big and broad-shouldered, he stood in road-dusty robes in front of their cart, cupping both hands around his mouth and shouting.

This was not going to end well. She'd been gone too long, made her father worry. She could hear it in his voice. Kirra would certainly be punished this time.

Unless . . .

As she approached, she could see that Taro had his back to the cart as he yelled into the forest. The two-wheeled contraption was in the middle of the road, directly under an overhanging tree branch. Their supplies were covered by a clump of soft robes and blankets.

Kirra leaped to that tree and found herself perched above his head. One of the talents she had discovered while traveling Outside was the ability to move silently.

"Kir-ra! Come back here this instant!" His voice was booming now that she was so close. "If I have to go into that forest, you can forget about coming on the next trip!"

As he was calling, Kirra stepped off the branch and

dropped directly onto the blankets in the cart. She quickly pulled a few of them over herself and started fake snoring. Loudly.

Taro whirled around, surprised, and whipped the blankets off of Kirra. "Where have you been, daughter?"

Kirra slowly blinked her eyes open and rubbed them with her fists. "Why, whatever do you mean, Paja?" she asked, her voice dripping with innocence. "I've been resting here the whole time." Kirra let out a huge yawn and made an exaggerated show of looking around at their surroundings. "Oh! Are we almost there?"

Taro just sighed and shook his head. "At least the Council chose my Helper well. I swear, you can sell a story better than anyone." He narrowed his eyes and shook a finger at her. "Even the flimsiest and sketchiest of stories."

Kirra giggled. Taro grabbed her around the waist with both hands and lifted her out of the cart as if she weighed no more than a small sack of papayas. Then he set her down and pointed at the bend in the road up ahead. "We're approaching Lukweii. You stay close to me now, understand?"

"Yes, Paja." Kirra sighed. "But there's just so much to *see* out here." She spread her arms and twirled in a circle, indicating the entire world. "I never have the chance to soak it all in before it's time to go back home."

"I know, little one, I know." He leaned down and kissed the top of her head. "But we have a job to do. It's time to get ready for the show!" Taro tapped both of his cheeks. "Go ahead . . . do your magic."

Kirra turned to the cart, rummaged around under the blankets, and came out with a small stool and a leather carrycase. Taro sat on the stool, eye to eye with his daughter.

Kirra pulled a small pouch from the case, dipped her fingers in, and they came out covered in a sticky black mixture of sap from a gum tree mixed with charcoal. Taro grimaced, baring his teeth at her, and Kirra rubbed the paste over three of his front teeth. When she was done, it looked like those teeth had fallen out, leaving a black space.

"Ach. I'll never get used to the taste of that."

"*Paja*. Don't talk. Let it dry."

He nodded obediently.

After that, she pulled out a battered eye patch and slipped it over Taro's head, settling the shabby fabric in place over his right eye.

Next, she dipped into another pouch filled with ashes mixed with a bit of water and powdered milk, and Kirra ran her fingers over Taro's head, giving his black curls a series of mangy gray streaks. She followed this up by grabbing a handful of hay and wedging some of the stalks into his mane, then rubbing her hands in the dirt before smudging them across her father's brown cheeks.

The final touch was to grab a lumpy pillow and a dark, threadbare cloak. Taro leaned forward and let Kirra drape the cloak over his shoulders and then shove the pillow underneath the collar of his robe so that it rested behind his neck, giving him the appearance of a hunchback.

"So?" He rose from the stool but remained slightly bent over, scowling. When he spoke, it was with the raspy yet powerful voice that he would use in the village. "How do I look?"

"Hideous."

"Perfect!" Taro indicated the cart with a nod of his head. "Now it's your turn."

Kirra sighed again and pulled a battered straw sun hat from the cart. She tied up her long, curly dark hair with a bit of string, then pushed it all up inside of the hat as she set it on her head. Afterward, she slipped on an oversize cloak and rubbed some of the dirt on her own face as well.

Taro tilted his head to study his daughter, then *tsk-tsk*ed at her.

"What's wrong?"

"You're becoming much too pretty to pull this off."

"*Paja.* Quit teasing. It'll be fine."

"I'm not teasing. You are growing into a beautiful and intelligent young woman, Kirra." Taro rubbed his chin as he studied her. "But we're stuck with this for today, and the show will start soon. You remember how to act, yes?"

"Of course." Kirra rolled her eyes. "Like Tiko. Grunt a lot, use very small words, breathe loudly while never quite closing my mouth, and constantly scratch myself in unseemly places."

Taro laughed but wagged his finger at her. "Okay, no more jokes, and I mean it. Time to go over the rules."

"Again?" Kirra could do this routine in her sleep.

"Yes, again. Now, what is your name?"

"Kala."

"And what is the one thing we never ever do?" Taro's voice was somber.

"Answer any questions about our real home."

"Such as?"

"Where it is, how long it would take to get there, what direction it's in, what it's like there, how many people live there."

Taro smiled. "That's my daughter."

"*No.* You can't say that, Paja. I'm your *son*, Kala." Kirra scratched herself in an unseemly place for emphasis.

Taro chuckled. "Point taken. Let's get moving." He reached into the cart for his cane and started to make his way down the dirt road, hunched over and favoring one leg.

Kirra backed herself in between the cart's two long handles, picked them off the ground, and placed them on her shoulders. Then she grunted with the effort of pulling it behind her.

Even burdened as she was now, Kirra was able to keep her head up and take in the surroundings as she followed

Taro down the road. This was so much better than being stuck at home doing chores, sweeping up their family's hut for the seventeenth time a day at her mother's insistence, or yet again gathering fuel for the community cook fires. Outside, there was something *new* everywhere she looked. Back in the familiar limits of Zedu, Kirra had already seen everything there was to see.

As they wound around the final bend and the walls of the village came into sight, the front gate swung open and a gaggle of kids came pouring out. Kirra watched them as they rushed up the road. Kids she had never met, many of them her own age. They had stories she hadn't heard a hundred times before, knew games she had never played, and ate food she had never tasted.

But, just like always, these kids did not have eyes for her. They swarmed around the hunchbacked Taro, who limp-marched resolutely toward the gate and pretended not to notice them.

"The Volcano Man! The Volcano Man!" the kids yelled as they escorted him to Lukweii's entrance. Kirra trudged along behind with the cart.

"The Volcano Man has come back!"

2

THE ANNUAL STORYTELLING CONTEST in Lukweii was held at the end of summer to celebrate a successful hunting season and harvest. The hard work of collecting food was done, and the whole village took a break before the labor of salting meat, preserving fruit, and storing grain for the winter was begun.

As everyone congregated in the huge common area in the center of the village—more people than Kirra had ever seen in one spot—she watched vendors push their way through the crowd, peddling roasted meat on sticks and bags of honeyed nuts. Parents bounced toddlers on their knees while clusters of friends drank deeply from wooden cups. Children close to Kirra's age marked the perimeter of the storytellers' circle, crammed shoulder to shoulder in the front row, leaning forward in eager anticipation.

Kirra watched from her vantage point at the rear of the crowd, where she had made a perch by piling up the blankets in the cart so she could see over the heads of the grown-ups. (Taro was off preparing for the contest, and there was absolutely no need for him to know that Kirra was working her way through a third bag of the delicious nuts.)

She sighed as she watched the huddled children jostling one another to get the position with the best view. Kirra wanted so badly to get right down in their jumbled ranks and join in the conversations. But she was under strict orders—when she and Taro encountered people Outside, it was her job to be forgettable, not to make friends. The only bad part about being her paja's Helper was that she had to hide everything that made her Kirra in order to be Kala, the Volcano Man's right hand. She didn't even like Kala. He was dull and unimaginative and kept to himself, while Kirra wanted to laugh and explore and connect.

Kirra sighed again. Someday Taro would trust her to keep the secrets of the Zedu. She just wanted that someday to hurry up and get here.

At last, the waiting for the celebration was almost done.

As dusk settled over the village, one of the elders waded through the mob and stepped into the storytellers' circle, carrying a torch. He bent over and touched it to the dried leaves and logs piled in the fire pit. Soon the faces of the children in the front row were glowing in the light of the dancing flames as the first storyteller entered the circle and began.

As this was the fourth contest in as many villages that Kirra had witnessed, she knew how it worked. The schedule was rigged so that the beginner tale spinners went first, and each person who came after had more experience, so the stories got better and better as the night wore on. As they all came from neighboring villages, the accents varied a bit, and some of the words—especially slang—were unfamiliar due to regional dialects. But she could mostly follow everything that everyone was saying. Besides, as her father had told her many times, it's not *what* you say but *how* you say it that really matters.

As Kirra sat atop the cart and munched on her snacks, she heard tales of romance and adventure and exploring. There were stories about traveling priestesses, and talking animals, and giant warriors, and ships that could rise up from the ocean and sail among the stars.

And always, saved for the grand finale, was the Volcano Man.

Kirra felt a familiar surge of pride as she watched her

father make his way to the center of the circle, but also a bundle of nerves buzzing in her stomach. Because some-day that would be her down there, with every stranger's eye trained on her expectantly.

The crowd went completely quiet as Taro stood in the center of the circle. He turned slowly, his "good" eye bor-ing into the mob, letting the silence stretch out until Kirra thought she was going to burst.

Finally, he began by tapping his cane on the ground. Softly at first, and then more and more insistently. "Under-neath your feet," he rasped, "right now, beneath this very village, there lives an army of angry fire demons."

Taro traced a circle around the perimeter of the storytelling space, rhythmically thumping his cane just a few inches from the wide-eyed kids in the front row. "It is in the demons' nature to burn . . . to consume . . . to destroy. Anything they can get their hands on becomes a charred and black nothing. Your beautiful home, your most cherished possessions"— Taro leaned forward, scowling, and stage-whispered into the face of a young girl—"even your loved ones."

Taro resumed his pacing. "And they can hear you down there, you know. Oh, aye, they can hear you very well. The pounding of your footsteps keeps them constantly awake and agitated, fueling their rage. So you would do well to remember this: Every time you bounce a ball, or play a game of tag, or enjoy yourself at a village dance, you are only stoking the demons' unquenchable desire for vengeance.

"Trust me, good people of Lukweii, each one of those demons would like nothing better than to escape from their underground prison"—Taro crept closer to the crowd—"and take their red-hot claws"—closer now—"and GRAB you!" Here Taro lunged at the nearest boy in the front row, thumping him in the chest with that cane. The boy screamed and scrambled backward to the laughter and jeers of his surrounding friends. Taro fixed one of those giggling youngsters with a stare. "Then they would drag you underground and slowly roast you alive." The boy's smirk faded as the flickering shadows played across Taro's scowling face.

Paja then launched into the backstory of these hideous creatures. How they used to be a proud race who lived aboveground—*just like the people of this very village*—but they displeased the gods so greatly with their greedy and violent ways that they were turned into fire demons and trapped underground for thousands of years.

But Kirra was only half listening to this part, which she knew by heart. Instead, she studied the faces of the villagers. She loved how everyone, not just the kids but also the adults throughout the crowd, reacted to Taro's words. Glancing uneasily at the ground, eyes growing wide, sharing a meaningful look with their neighbor, gasping in surprise. Taro had all of them on an invisible leash and was leading them right where he wanted them to go, just like always.

When Taro bent down to scoop up a handful of dirt, she started paying attention to him again. Her favorite part was coming up.

". . . and so, at the end of the day, what is protecting any of us?" Taro looked at his fist, where he was letting the dust sift through his fingers to blow away on the breeze. "A few feet of dirt. Just a thin crust between you and the legion of powerful supernatural creatures that want nothing more than to destroy you and everyone you know."

Taro was quiet for several moments, letting that threat sink in. When he spoke again, it was nearly a whisper, and the entire village had to lean in to hear.

"But there are certain places, my friends . . . places too frightening even to think about . . . places where the fire demons are able to escape their underground prison and come out into the light of day."

Taro fell silent once again, and Kirra could hear the word as it was passed through the crowd in hushed tones.

Volcanoes.

"I have traveled far, and I have seen these spaces where the fire demons have beaten so hard against the roof of their prison that great cracks in the land have opened right up."

Taro shook his head sadly. "The gods have tried to help. They build great mountains on top of these Earth scars, attempting to keep a lid on the boiling cauldron of malevolence that threatens us all."

Another dramatic pause. Kirra studied his technique, what Taro was doing to get the timing just right. Because she could practically feel the entire assembly holding their collective breath for the next part.

Her father sighed heavily. "But even the gods have their limitations, my friends. And the seething hatred of the fire demons is so potent, sometimes nothing can be done to keep it from bubbling over and scorching the land."

Whoosh!

The bonfire exploded, the flames leaping twenty, thirty, forty feet in the air. The entire village circle was made bright as noon for a moment, and Kirra could feel the flash of heat on her face even though she was way in the back. People screamed and covered their eyes, then laughed nervously at the reactions of their neighbors.

Kirra knew that Taro had slipped a hand into his cloak during the buildup to the big moment, gathered a handful of highly flammable powder, and tossed it into the fire while he was gesturing during his story. She also knew he was now preparing for his next trick.

"What happens then is more destructive than anything you have ever seen. Nay, anything you have ever imagined. For when the chaos of the Underworld is unleashed, nothing can stand in its path. Why, the heat gets so intense . . ."

Taro paused and snatched up a smallish rock from the ground.

". . . the heat gets so intense, the very stones of the land melt and form puddles."

As he was saying this, Taro's fist closed over the rock. A thick goo dripped through his fingers and splattered on the ground. The crowd gasped.

Kirra grinned. While the exploding bonfire was bigger and showier, she appreciated the melting rock trick more. First, you had to retrieve the packet of goo from your pocket and subtly cup it in your palm without anyone noticing. Then you had to send the rock sliding down your sleeve without making any unnatural movements. Finally, you had to time the dripping of the goo with the disappearance of the rock so they looked like one and the same. She had been practicing for six months and was just now getting to the point where she could pull off the trick. Well, kind of. With very small pebbles, anyway.

"The flame races like a river, cascading down the sides of the volcano and streaming across the fields." Taro resumed the narrative, using hand gestures and sweeps of his cane to emphasize the power of the mighty volcano. "There is no way to stop it. The entire village, and everyone in it, would simply . . . be . . . gone."

Taro shook his head sadly. "The only solution, my friends, is to stay far, far away from any volcano. Do not build anything you care about anywhere near its cursed base, and—if you value your life—do not even go hiking near one of these blights on our land. A volcano is a dark place, my friends . . . a place where the gods have failed."

Even though Taro altered the details of the fire demons saga each year, the conclusion was always the same. A collective shiver went through the crowd at his final words, and all were silent as they watched her father, his head bowed reverently. Kirra was confident that this had been another successful contest. The only thing left to do now was load up the cart with their winnings—sacks of grain, salted meats, and crop seeds—and start the trek homeward in the morning. Kirra stretched her arms over her head and yawned. It would be good to get a few hours' sleep before their journey.

"But what of the Takers?" someone yelled, shattering the silence. "Will no one tell a story about them?"

Kirra's head snapped back to the festival. No one ever interrupted the finale of a storytelling contest.

She watched as a man jumped up from where he was seated in the crowd and marched right into the storytellers' circle. The style and color of his robes marked him as another outsider, a visitor from a neighboring village, perhaps.

Taro backed away from the intruder, his eyes searching for Kirra in the crowd.

The newcomer pointed at Taro while he stared out at the assembled villagers. "You would sit here and listen to fairy tales instead of a true warning." He shook his head. "I don't have any fancy tricks. I can't make the fire dance up into the night sky or turn rocks into liquid. All I can do is relate what I have seen with my own eyes."

Taro was still scanning the crowd, and Kirra waved to him. Spotting her, he exited the circle and made his way through the crowd as quickly as he could, elbowing people roughly out of the way. Kirra had never seen her father do anything like that.

"The Takers—they came last year to the fishing village where I grew up," the strange man continued. "Arrived on great ships. We had never seen anything like them."

The village elder who had lit the bonfire to start the festivities entered the circle, flanked by two strong men. "The contest is over, my friend," he said, motioning for the newcomer to follow him out of the circle.

But the new storyteller ignored them, facing the crowd and raising his voice. "These Takers. They are *monstrous*. In the space of just a few months, they had overrun my beloved village, enslaved my people." His voice shook with emotion. "They took everything. I barely escaped."

Kirra scrunched up her eyebrows in confusion. What kind of a story was this? She scanned the faces of the crowd and could tell the villagers were thinking the same thing. Instead of the rapt expressions she'd seen during Taro's tales, she saw people glancing around at one another, looking a little nervous or uncomfortable. A few young children started crying.

The village elder and his two strong friends closed in on the man, but he backed away, his voice frantic now. "You must listen!" the man cried. "Please! I did not come here to entertain. I came to issue a warning. You must listen, and you must act. All of you."

Kirra jumped in surprise when Taro grabbed her by the arm, so wrapped up in the ranting of this strange man that she had lost track of her father in the crowd. "Gather your things," Taro said through clenched teeth. "We're leaving."

"Now?" Kirra said. "What about the prize?"

"You know we don't need it. Now let's go."

"But we've never left this early—"

"*Now*, Kirra." Taro spoke in his sternest Volcano Man voice. There was no arguing with that.

He started pulling the cart away before Kirra had even jumped down from her perch. The man in the circle rushed to finish his tale before he was caught up and forcibly removed. "I escaped to a village near here, on the south side of the volcano. Nafaluu. You must have heard of it. Near the waterfall, yes? The cliffs? A beautiful place." His voice rose to a shout. "And I am here to tell you that a group of Takers was spotted in the area just last month. They are spreading! Please hear me, good people, the Takers have come!"

"Don't listen to him." Taro's voice was a sheet of ice.

The cart was nearly to the village gates, but Kirra craned her neck to look back over her shoulder. The man was shouting now as he was being dragged away. "You must not let the Takers anywhere near here! You must be vigilant and protect yourselves. Or your village will be the next to be taken!"

3

THE NEXT MORNING, Kirra awoke to birdsong in her ears and sunlight warm on her face. The cart was gently rocking as Taro pulled it along the path. He strode upright, the cane no longer in his hands, and his gait was sure and strong. She lifted her head out of the tangle of blankets and saw that they were nearly home.

"Paja? Did you walk all night?"

"Aye," Taro said without turning around.

Kirra stretched and yawned, then climbed out of the

blankets, hopped down to the ground, and fell into step beside him, working the kinks out of her sleepy legs. The eye patch and the tooth black and the dirt were all gone. The Volcano Man was just her father again.

"Do you want me to take a turn pulling the cart?"

"No, that's okay, little one." Taro finally looked over at her and offered a shadow of a smile. "It's a lot easier now that you're out of it. Did you get some good sleep?"

Kirra nodded. They walked along in silence for a while, the sun rising higher in the sky and growing warmer on her patches of bare skin. She wasn't sure how to ask him what she wanted to. As she had drifted off to sleep, all she could think about was the look on his face as he had grabbed her and hustled her out of the village while that man told his strange tale.

Finally she broached the subject. "Paja . . . ?"

"Yes, my dear?"

"That strange story last night . . . you don't think . . . I mean, there's no chance any of that was true, right?"

"It doesn't matter." The smile faded from Taro's eyes. "A story is true if people believe it. You know that."

"Got it." That was a relief. "So he's just doing what we do, then. Right?"

Taro gave her a look. "How do you mean?"

"He's making up scary stories so people will stay away from that village. Nafaluu."

Taro set his jaw and shifted his eyes back to the road ahead. "Perhaps."

"Because he talked about the settlement by the cliffs, with the waterfall behind it. That's where we went on my first trip Outside, remember? It was sooooo pretty. And there were no weird Taker people there."

"That was a year ago, Kirra."

"Wait—so you think maybe what he was talking about was really *true* true? Not just story true?"

It was a long time before Taro answered. "I don't know, Kirra. Much can happen in a year."

"But what if he—?"

"We'll talk no more about it just now." Taro sighed. He turned to look at her again, placed a hand on his daughter's shoulder. "I'm sorry if that came out with a sharp tone. I just need some time to think, aye? We will discuss it again before we go Outside the next time."

Kirra placed her hand on top of his. It was warm and reassuring. Just like always. "Okay, Paja."

It was easy to put it out of her mind just then, because she recognized the slow curve their path was taking as it followed the river, and she knew that just on the other side of it was Zedu.

That was a warm and reassuring feeling, too. Because as much as she enjoyed being Outside, she had to admit that she also liked coming home. Sure, she had seen many interesting things and people. But she loved her own friends and family. Yes, even Tiko.

As they rounded that bend in the path, the volcano rose dramatically from the ground in front of them. Clouds of smoke drifted out of the crater way up at the top, making it look like the volcano was on the verge of erupting and spewing molten lava all over the surrounding fields at any moment.

"I wonder who's on smoke duty this morning," she said.

"Probably the Calla twins."

Kirra had to grin at that. The Zedu elders had chosen well when giving that job to the twins. Keeping the fires stoked just inside the rim of the volcano all through the day and night was a long and potentially boring task. But the twins were inseparable, and they kept each other company the whole time with no complaints. And if one of them snuck a nap on the job, well, the other one was there to take care of things.

She was glad she hadn't been chosen to be a Helper for smoke duty. It would be so dull to sit in the same exact spot all the time. But as she looked at the crater, hundreds of feet above their heads, she had to admit that at least the view would be spectacular.

Kirra breathed deeply and smiled. It was good to be back, and she couldn't wait to tell Tiko about the strange story she'd heard in Lukweii. Kirra and her father marched along toward their big, beautiful volcano home.

4

AS SHE TRUDGED UP the steep slope with her father, Kirra
scanned the hillside's thickets of brush and jumbles of rock
formations. Even though she had approached from the
Outside multiple times now, her trained eye simply could
not find the hidden entrance. Was it there, by the sagebrush
and the . . . ? No, that was just a trick of shadow and light.
Kirra held a hand above her eyes to block out the sun and
squinted as she made her way up the volcano wall. Could it
be over there, behind that gnarled scrub pine? Maybe, but
then why wasn't—

"Gotcha!"

Kirra let out a squeal as she was grabbed around the waist. She spun around to find her friend Tatuu, who had slipped out of a crack in the hillside surrounded by a clump of thorny bushes. The girl threw back her head and laughed, her unruly nest of hair flopping all over. "The look on your face gets better every time."

Kirra placed a hand over her racing heart and blew out a stream of air. "If you keep doing that, I might just stop coming home altogether."

"Girls, hush now." Kuzo, one of the official Watchers at this post, peeked his head out of the narrow opening in the rock wall and shook a finger at Tatuu. "A good Helper should know better. Come inside." He beckoned them forward and nodded at Kirra's father. "Welcome back, Taro. You must be glad to be safely home after your travels."

Taro made a fist and touched it to his forehead. "Zedu provides," he said in greeting.

As Kirra slipped through the crack and made her way through the twisting tunnel carved into the rock, she once again marveled at how so many Zeduans, even the grown-ups, seemed intimidated by the prospect of going Outside. It gave her a little thrill of self-satisfaction to know that she had seen things that few of them ever would.

But as she emerged from the tunnel onto a ledge inside

the volcano crater, she had to admit it was good to be back home. One of the benefits of traveling Outside was being able to see Zedu through fresh eyes whenever she returned, and feelings of awe and pride reawakened each time. The morning sunlight filtered through the opening far above, softly illuminating the intricate levels of terraces that made up their concealed community. Dozens of great overlapping ridges carved into the rock rose over her head and fell away beneath her, like a giant's spiral staircase. Some had groupings of huts for the various clans in little villages, others supported land for crops or livestock or places of gathering. And far below, at the very bottom of the volcano's interior, was the pool of fresh springwater that served as the lifeblood of the community.

But Kirra didn't have time to dwell on the amazing architectural accomplishments of countless generations of Zeduan people, because Tiko spotted her right away. He must have been scoping out the hidden entrance since sunup, waiting all morning for their return.

"Kirra!" He raced over and tugged at her cloak. "How was the Outside this time?" he asked eagerly.

"Oh, you know"—she shrugged as casually as possible— "it was pretty good, I guess." Kirra faked a big yawn.

"Stop teasing!" Tiko put his hands on his hips. "Was it amazing? Tell me!"

Kirra broke into a grin. "You got me. It was completely amazing." She gave him a sly sidelong glance. "I caught a squirrel this time."

"Wow! Lemme see it!" Tiko dove for the pouch tied to her belt, grabbing at it with both hands.

Kirra pushed his arms away. "I don't have it anymore. I felt bad for taking it from its home, so I let it go."

Tiko crossed his arms and huffed. "You didn't catch any squirrel."

Kirra's grin got wider. "So that means you believe they do exist?"

"No."

"If I get another one, do you want me to bring it back?"

"Yes!"

They both laughed. Tiko looked over at where their father was still talking to Kuzo at the entrance and lowered his voice to a whisper. "Did you talk to him about me going with you next time?"

Kirra tousled his hair affectionately. One of the things she admired about her brother was that he didn't share the usual Zeduan fear of everything beyond the crater walls. Tiko was *dying* to get Outside someday. "Oh, Tiko. You know he won't even think about it until you get to Helper age."

His shoulders slumped. "It's not fair."

Kirra glanced back at Taro, still tied up in conversation. "But I did bring something that might cheer you up. . . ."

"Really? What is it?" Tiko was back at her, jumping up like a puppy. "Show me!"

She laughed and untied the pouch. "First, I got you a little treat." She pulled out a sack of honeyed nuts, which he accepted eagerly. "Hide those from Maja or she'll only let you have two or three at a time."

"Oh, I will. Thanks, Kirra!"

"And I brought you something else . . ." She glanced around conspiratorially. "If you can keep a *really* big secret . . ."

Tiko's eyes went wide. "No way," he breathed. "You found more?"

Kirra nodded. She reached back into the pouch and slowly removed her fist. With a dramatic flourish learned from watching her Storyteller father, she unfurled her fingers to reveal the three rough arrowheads she'd found while walking next to a creek. Kirra dropped the gifts into Tiko's open palm, and he went silent as he studied them.

War and weapons were foreign concepts in Zedu. The only knowledge of battle their people had was from the stories Taro told around the cook fires when he visited the various clans in the community. Kirra knew these stories were meant to be cautionary tales, examples of what could happen to their society if they stopped cooperating. But the taboo nature of the subject had the opposite effect on Tiko and his friends. They were fascinated with all the epic battles that no doubt must be raging somewhere Outside, and they secretly played Zeduan Warrior when no grown-ups were looking.

He lifted the biggest arrowhead and turned it this way and that. "These are incredible. Thank you so much, Kirra!"

She gave him a stern look. "Now, you'd better hide those even better than you do the treats, understand? Or we'll both be in trouble."

Tiko nodded reverentially. Then his face lit up. "I have the perfect place! My secret spot. Come with me—I'll show you."

Kirra called to her father, "I'll look after Tiko. We'll be home in time for lunch." Taro waved at her, and she hustled to join her brother.

She smirked at the idea of a "secret spot." Pretty much every nook and cranny of the volcano's interior had been mapped out years ago. Nothing was truly hidden in Zedu—there simply wasn't enough room for secrets.

They neared the end of the ledge where they had entered the volcano's interior, but Tiko ran past the stone staircase carved into the crater wall. There were many ways other than the stairs to get from one broad terrace to another: You could rappel down on climber's ropes, or take the crank-powered wooden elevator, but Tiko preferred to—

"Woo-hoo!" he yelled as he leaped straight off the edge and plunged to a cushion of moss and leaves waiting below. Kirra rolled her eyes, yet she had to admit as she made the same jump that it was fun to feel her stomach flip-flop as her body rushed through the open air.

She popped up from the soft pile and had to jog to keep pace with Tiko as they circled the volcano's towering walls, heading to his hideaway.

Kirra waved to people as they rushed past. There was Meena, one of her old teachers, playing with a group of small children in front of her hut. And there was Samos, who delivered fresh milk each morning from the goat pens. And a group of Builders and their Helpers, patching up a suspension bridge that spanned two prominent terraces. It was comforting to watch the Zeduans care for their home and for one another. As Kirra got older, she took in more details about how the community functioned. Everything was in balance. Her people lived in harmony with each other and the resources that the volcano provided.

Tiko had clambered up a series of staircases until he was more than three-fourths of the way to the rim of the crater. Kirra, not well rested from her all-night journey in the cart, found herself wheezing as she tried to keep pace.

She looked up to see her brother beckoning to her. He had stopped at the base of one of the Courier zip-line stations.

By the time she made it up to that terrace, Tiko had flopped on the ground, panting, and was watching the Couriers. The station—one of six evenly spaced around the interior of Zedu—was a wooden platform up on eight-foot supports. Zip-line cables radiated out like spokes of a wheel, connected to various terraces clear across the other side of the volcano.

A Zeduan citizen who needed to send something to a different clan brought it to the station and dropped it off. Then a Courier put it in a pouch, secured themself in a harness attached to a zip line, and stepped off the platform that extended right out over the lip of the terrace, hundreds of feet above the ground below. The result was an exhilarating ride through the air to the delivery spot.

Tiko watched, rapt, as another Courier stepped off into nothingness and in mere seconds was no bigger to the eye than a dot, zooming halfway across the vast volcano.

Kirra sat down and nudged Tiko. "That would be the perfect job for someone I know. . . ."

"It would be fun," Tiko admitted. "But you know I want to be a Builder."

They sat there for a moment, catching their breath. "Well," Kirra finally said as she looked around, "aren't you going to take me to your hiding place?"

Tiko put a finger to his lips. He was watching the activity on the platform closely. "We have to wait until they're all busy. . . ."

A few moments later, a man climbed the steps and approached a Helper, while another Helper assisted a Courier with her harness straps. There were no other Couriers or

Helpers to take notice of the two kids down below. Tiko jumped up, grabbed Kirra's hand, and pulled her underneath the wooden stairs. They raced along below the Courier platform, made it to the rock wall where the structure was secured, and then Tiko wedged himself into a crack in the wall and disappeared.

Kirra was impressed. Tiko *had* actually managed to find a hidden nook. And the positioning of the Courier station would keep prying eyes away from it. Clever.

When she followed him into a sort of cave that formed a little room, she was even more impressed. Using material that was clearly left over from various construction projects, he and his friends had built tables and chairs, a couple of hammocks, and even a target board for a game of rolly darts.

"Wow, Tiko. This is nice! The Builders would be crazy not to take you when you're old enough."

"Thanks!" Tiko beamed at the praise. "It took us forever to sneak in all the supplies." He stood on tiptoe to retrieve a wooden box from a little shelf of rock and stashed his arrowheads inside. "It's been easier lately, because all the grown-ups are getting ready for the harvest festival."

"Oh, that's right. I forgot about that." Kirra had been away a little longer than she'd realized.

"I never forget about that—it's my favorite time of year."

"You like it more than your birthday?"

"*Way* more. The grown-ups are always so busy during the

day, and then they go to bed early and sleep hard all night. Us kids can do whatever we want!"

Kirra smiled and shook her head. She should have known.

Tiko tugged on her cloak again. "Now, tell me all about your adventures this time! Don't leave anything out. And *no teasing.*"

Kirra laughed. "I promise." They cuddled up in one of the hammocks, and she told him everything she could remember. When she listed the animals Paja had pointed out to her as they hiked along, Tiko peppered her with questions about the beasts they'd had to hide from, especially the crocodiles. She told him about a place on the riverbank where the water was so wide you could hardly see the other side. She described what it was like to almost lose yourself in a real forest. She reported on what the kids were wearing in distant villages, along with what games they were playing.

When she finally tired of answering all of Tiko's eager questions, she yawned and stretched. "We should be getting back. I know Maja will want to know where we are." Tiko grumbled a bit before reluctantly agreeing. Then they snuck out from under the Courier platform and made their way home.

The huts were arranged in a semicircle that formed a courtyard where the children could be watched by all the parents of their clan. Kirra became a bit nostalgic for the times before she was a Helper, when there were countless hours to play out here with all her friends.

The courtyard was empty at midday, however, with everyone either off at school or doing their jobs around the community. Maybe she could sneak in a nap before—

"Kirra!" Her mother burst from the hut and came straight for her. "You're here! You're safe!" Djiahna grabbed Kirra in a fierce hug, pulled back, and held her by the shoulders to study her face, then hugged her tightly again. "You are safe."

Wow. Kirra knew Maja was perpetually nervous when her daughter was on the Outside, but this welcome seemed . . . different somehow. A little more frantic than usual.

Kirra looked over Djiahna's shoulder at Tiko, let her tongue hang out the side of her mouth, and made a face like she was being suffocated to death. "Yes, Maja," she croaked. Tiko giggled.

Taro stepped out of the hut, and Kirra glanced over at him. She furrowed her brow. Paja was usually very relaxed after returning home, but right now his eyes looked clouded with concern. . . . Was something going on?

Djiahna finally stopped hugging Kirra so tightly, but she still held on to her daughter's shoulders as she stepped back to study her. "Oh my, you look thin, my dear. When was the last time you ate? Were you warm enough at night?" She glanced at her spouse. "Taro, why is she covered in grime?

Don't you ever make sure she washes when you go wandering about? I know for good and certain that there are plenty of lakes and streams in the Outside. Has no other village managed to invent soap?"

"All is well, Maja," Kirra said.

Djiahna studied her, eyebrows scrunched up. "Sometimes I worry that you are becoming just as good as your father at telling stories. . . ."

"But that's the plan, Maja."

Djiahna finally broke into a smile and hugged her again. "I suppose it is. Come in, there's some stew left over. I'll warm it up for you."

Kirra and Tiko walked into the hut. Taro put a comforting arm around Djiahna as they followed. Her mother was whispering, but Kirra could still make out the words. "You promise that no one saw the two of you . . . no one who shouldn't have?"

Taro whispered in return, his tone pleasant, "No, my love. It was a good trip. Very successful." He nodded in Kirra's direction. "You would be proud of our daughter. She is learning quickly. Someday she will be a fine Storyteller."

Kirra's heart glowed with the recognition from her father, but it was short-lived, as she couldn't help but think that something was not quite right between her parents.

Lunch was served, and the family talked and laughed and reveled in being reunited once again. But Kirra kept an eye on her parents. The little secret glances they gave each other. The sleep circles under Paja's eyes. The worry lines around Maja's eyes and the way her mouth, usually so smiley, kept turning down at the corners.

Kirra sighed. Grown-ups. They always thought they were being so secretive. But they never were. When would they realize kids weren't stupid?

Kirra decided she'd find out exactly what was going on.

5

KIRRA LIFTED THE TOP OFF the great wicker basket, climbed inside, and got down on her knees, then carefully eased the lid back into place. Long ago, she had made a small hole in the basket at eye level, and through it she gazed out at the little grove of banyan trees in the center of the courtyard.

And she waited.

She felt a twinge of guilt about eavesdropping. But it quickly passed. After all, if her parents didn't want her to listen in on their private conversations, then they shouldn't have them in the same place every time.

And they shouldn't be hiding important things from her anyway. She understood the need to have secrets around Tiko, especially if they were about things that affected the whole community. He wouldn't understand, and he might share them with his group of friends. But Kirra was an official Helper now. She had been Outside four different times! Someday she would be entrusted with keeping her people safe by spreading stories about the fire demons, and also with keeping the lore and legends of Zeduan history alive, just like her father. She had worked hard and deserved to hear about anything that was going on.

Just when her legs had started to cramp, her parents finally appeared, brushing aside the bamboo curtain at the back entrance to the family hut. Kirra saw Maja scan the courtyard for anyone who might be about, but at this time of the evening, everyone had likely finished up dinner and was now busy with festival preparations down in the village square. Luckily, Maja didn't think it necessary to check inside the wicker basket.

"So," Taro said, "there were more sightings? In just the three weeks we were gone?"

Kirra watched through the little hole as her mother nodded. "Once on the steppe over on the southeastern side—a group of them driving cattle. And again a few days later, near the river. We can't be certain, of course, but it looked like they were surveying a good spot for a bridge, if you can imagine that. Then a third time, only the day before you got home. There were three of them, and it looked . . ." She took a shaky breath. "It looked like a scouting party of some sort. Poking around, spying, writing on a large parchment. Like they were making a map!"

Djiahna brushed away a tear with the sleeve of her robe. Paja held her close. Then she started again in a stronger voice. "Taro, that last one was the worst. I was expecting your return at any moment, and they were so near the trail you always take. When I got the report, I was certain you and Kirra were going to run right into them."

"I'm sorry you were worried, my love. Does anyone else know about the sightings?"

Djiahna shook her head. "The Watchers report directly to the Elder Council. They are sworn to secrecy."

Kirra wondered what she could be talking about. Maja was a Helper for the Council, and so most of the secrets of the tribe were shared with her. In just a few years, Djiahna would be eligible to be elected to an official position on the Council itself, and then she would know everything there was to know about Zedu.

It wasn't usually big news when people were spotted in the vicinity. Sometimes Outsiders wandered by the volcano as a matter of course. It was to be expected. And that was the job of the Watchers: to track their movements and let the

Council know when they had safely passed. So why were her parents so worried now that—

"And the Watchers were sure it was them?"

Djiahna scoffed. "With the way they look, could they be mistaken for anything else? Plus, they're so big and clumsy and loud. Trust me, the Watchers are certain."

Taro shook his head slowly, worry lines creasing his face. "In the last village we were in, Lukweii, a man was spreading terrible stories about them. They fit with what we've been hearing for months now. He called them the Takers."

Kirra put a hand over her mouth to smother a gasp. The Takers were real? Why hadn't Paja told her when she'd asked about them?

Djiahna harrumphed. "*Takers.* A perfect name for them."

"And there's more. This man said that . . ." Taro took a deep breath. "He said that they had been spotted in Nafaluu."

Djiahna's eyes went wide, and her hand covered her heart. "So close?" Taro nodded. "What are we going to do?"

"We are Zedu. We continue as we always have. I spread the stories and our people stay safely out of sight."

"But, Taro, how long can that last? How long until we realize we may have to defend ourselves? Just like everyone else on Maja Earth who has something worth fighting for."

Kirra had to stifle another gasp. *Fighting?* It was like hearing Maja use a profanity.

Her father looked as surprised as Kirra felt. "Surely there is not talk on the Council of war?"

"Of course there is," Djiahna whispered fiercely, even though no one else was in the courtyard. She pulled out of her husband's embrace. "What we have here is special, Taro. You have traveled, so you know this better than anyone."

"But fighting goes against everything our people believe in." He threw his hands into the air. "If we fight, we'll no longer have what we've built here! All would be lost even if we won."

Kirra was chewing on her lip so hard she could taste blood. She wasn't sure what was more unsettling—this talk of fighting and the Takers, or seeing her parents disagree so strongly.

"Have you ever considered, Taro, that there will come a time when we don't have a choice in the matter?"

"Of course I have, but that doesn't mean—"

"How many generations do you imagine will live here in peace, undiscovered? Nothing lasts forever. Zedu must adapt in order to survive."

Taro's shoulders slumped. "But at what cost?"

Djiahna turned and strode to the porch, then looked back at her husband. "I don't want our homes—our children—to be *taken*. And if I have any voice on the Council, I will not allow it." She stormed into the hut, the bamboo curtain clacking in her wake.

Kirra had never seen Taro so sad. She hadn't given much thought to his feelings before, to be honest. But at that moment, she saw him as a whole person—not just her father—and he had a look of such utter defeat on his face, it broke her heart.

Taro walked slowly into the hut, and that's when Kirra heard Maja calling her name. Not good. She had to get inside without being discovered back here. Kirra stood too quickly, and a flare of pain shot through her cramped legs in protest. The wicker basket fell over, and Kirra rolled out into the dust. She staggered up, set the basket right, and ran around the hut to the front porch.

"Kirra!"

"I'm right here, Maja."

Djiahna pulled her hair back and quickly tied it in place, then straightened her robes, all business. "I have a Council meeting to attend. Your father is going to see if he can assist with any festival preparations, and I will need to join him when I'm free. You will have to watch Tiko until we get back."

"Yes, Maja." She didn't dare argue with Djiahna, not after she'd seen the fire in her eyes just moments ago.

Half an hour later, both of her parents were gone and Tiko was playing ball with his friends in the courtyard as Kirra watched from the hammock on the back porch. Her brother was laughing and yelling, chasing the frayed rope ball and kicking up mini dust storms. How nice it would be to have just one more day of being free of worries or responsibilities. Little kids could do whatever they . . .

Kirra sat up in the hammock. What was it Tiko had said? The grown-ups would all be consumed with festival preparations, so the kids could do whatever they wanted. It was true—her parents were either going to work through the night or come home so exhausted that they just collapsed into bed. Kirra could do whatever she wanted.

So what did she want to do? That was easy: First, she wanted to help protect Zedu. Always. But second, she wanted to make sure her parents never had the kind of disagreement she had just witnessed. Watching her mother and father talk like that to each other had disturbed her in a way she was not willing to examine. It was too scary.

The only way to do those two things was to learn the truth about the Takers. She would have to go to Nafaluu and see for herself. If they truly posed a threat, she could convince Paja to take action. She wouldn't be able to tell him she had been there, of course, but she would think of something. And if the stories about the Takers were just rumors, as she more than half expected, then she wouldn't have to do anything. All this talk and worry would just blow right through like a warm summer breeze on the steppe. And her parents would never have to fight about fighting again.

She needed to start building a story of her own. A story

that would prove she could be a real Storyteller. To do that, she would need to leave the cozy confines of Zedu—alone—and observe the Takers.

Her pulse raced at the thought. But in a good way. Her father had often told her, *You'll know your first story idea when it comes to you. You'll* feel *it.* She was definitely feeling this.

The waterfall near the village of Nafaluu was only an hour's walk from the secret exit tunnel on the east side of the crater. She could leave after everyone had fallen asleep, race over there, see what she needed to see, and be back in plenty of time to remain undiscovered. And she could finally be of real service to Zedu. After all, a good Storyteller didn't just have to know how to weave tales—she also had to know where to find them.

Kirra's mind was made up. She would leave tonight.

6

KIRRA'S HEART WAS THUMPING as she made her way through the doorway slowly and gently so the bamboo curtain wouldn't clack. She realized she was more afraid of getting caught by her mother and father than she was of being Outside all alone. But she had heard their sleep breathing, even heavier than normal, when passing by their private quarters. Those two were definitely out for the night.

She tiptoed down the wooden porch steps, skipping the creaky one. Scanning the courtyard, she was relieved to see that no one was out. Tiko had been right—all the grown-ups were just as exhausted as Taro and Djiahna after a full day of festival preparations.

It was quiet and still. Which made it that much harder not to scream when the lid of the wicker basket came flying off and Tiko popped his head out.

"I knew it!" he whispered fiercely.

"Shh!" Kirra made a *keep it down* gesture and pointed at the hut.

"You've been acting weird all evening," Tiko said a little more quietly. "I *knew* you were up to something."

"It's nothing." Kirra shook her head. "I just . . . I left something . . . you know, in your secret spot. I have to sneak back there and pick it up."

Tiko pointed to the knapsack Kirra was wearing. "Then why did I see you packing leftovers, a map, and your cutting stone?"

Kirra sighed. What kind of a Storyteller was she going to be if she couldn't even lie convincingly to her brother?

Tiko leaned forward, eyes wide. "You're going *Outside*, aren't you?"

Kirra realized there was no way out but straight through. "Okay, yes, I am. But it's only for a few hours. I'll be home before anyone wakes up." She glanced back at the dark windows of the hut. "But you can't tell Maja and Paja. You promise?"

"Of course I promise."

Whew. "Thank you so much, Tiko. If they found—"

"Because I'm going with you." He clambered out of the basket, then reached back inside and pulled out a knapsack of his own. "I'm already packed!"

"No way," Kirra said. "Not going to happen."

"Then you're not going, either." He turned toward the hut, cupped his hands around his mouth, and took an exaggerated breath, as if preparing to yell.

Kirra clamped her hand over his face. "You wouldn't."

Tiko nodded slowly. He totally would.

She sighed again and removed her hand.

"Come on, Kirra," Tiko pleaded. "I'll be good, I promise. I could even help you."

Kirra chewed her lip and looked around the dark courtyard. She wasn't going to get as good a chance as this again. And with Tiko apparently watching her every move, she might never even *get* another chance. She reluctantly concluded that he was right—she was going with him or not at all.

She fixed him with a stare. "Rule number one is that you do everything I say." Tiko grinned and nodded so hard it looked like he was trying to shake something out of his hair. "And rule number two is that you—"

"Do everything you say. I got it. Really and truly, Kirra. You can trust me."

A few moments later, they were creeping from terrace to

terrace, hugging the interior rock wall to stay in the shadows. Their stealth was unnecessary, though. All was quiet throughout Zedu. It was a boring night for the Watchers on duty.

When they neared the eastern exit, Kirra put a finger to her lips and motioned for Tiko to crouch behind a stack of firewood. "When I give the signal, you race straight for the tunnel. No stopping or looking back, understand?"

Tiko nodded solemnly.

Kirra reached into her knapsack and withdrew a stone, then threw it underhand so it rolled after it hit the ground, clattering noisily. Next she ducked down behind the firewood with Tiko and peeked over the top of the stack.

A moment later, a Watcher emerged from the crack in the wall to investigate the noise. As soon as he was far enough away with his back turned to them, Kirra grabbed Tiko's hand and they raced into the tunnel together, twisting this way and that through its curves. Then they popped out under the vast night sky.

Just like that. As on her previous trips with Paja, it felt exhilarating. But she knew they couldn't stop to take in the moonlit landscape. The Watcher would be back in just a moment, and things were much brighter out here. She tightened her grip on Tiko's hand and had to pull him hard to get him moving, as his mouth was agape and his head was on a swivel as he got his first unobstructed view of all the stars in the night sky. She led him up a path on the outside of the volcano that curved above the secret entrance and away from the gaze of the Watcher. They would head diagonally toward the rim of the crater for a while, then loop their way back down to the base, and, finally, across the plains toward Nafaluu.

This was real. They were doing it.

The going was a bit slow as Tiko—his head permanently craned upward—stumbled over rocks or stepped into holes as they waded through the tall grass of the plains.

"Watch where you're going, birdbrain," Kirra whispered as she caught his elbow and set him upright once again.

"I'm sorry, I just . . ." He spread out his arms to indicate the night sky. "I've never lived without walls, you know?"

It was hard for Kirra to stay annoyed, as she knew exactly what he was talking about. On her first trip Outside, Taro had let her ride in the cart almost the entire time so that she could simply take everything in.

As for this journey, Kirra was using the stars to navigate as she had been taught. She also periodically stopped to study the map—one of Paja's—by the moonlight. If a group of "Takers" was actually camped out near the village of Nafaluu, then, she figured, there was only one place they could be: a lone copse of woods by a bend in the river about a twenty-minute walk north of the waterfall.

And, if her calculations were correct, they should be getting close. In fact, that dark clump of vegetation rising up from the plains ahead of them was likely the spot.

She stopped Tiko and put her hands on his shoulders. "I need you to really listen to me," she whispered. "I know you are very clever, and starting now, I need you to act like you do when you're sneaking to your secret spot, okay? Very quiet and alert."

Tiko nodded solemnly. He mouthed, *I promise*, to demonstrate how quiet he could be.

"We're going to tiptoe over to that group of trees"—she pointed to the woods in the distance—"and we're going to see if there are some people camped out there."

"What people?"

"I'm not sure. There might not even be any. But if there are, we need to count them and get a quick sense of what their camp is like, and that's all. As soon as we do that, we're going to hustle right back home and get into bed."

Tiko nodded some more. "And why are we doing this?"

Kirra slowly touched a fist to her forehead, hoped that the gravity of the situation would sink into Tiko's brain. "We protect Zedu."

"Are these . . ." His eyes went wide. "Are they bad people?"

She wasn't sure how to answer. When the strange man in Lukweii had described the Takers, Kirra thought he was making everything up. But when Maja spoke in such worried tones, it had made Kirra think twice.

She frowned. What could Zeduans actually learn about Outsiders when they stayed within the crater walls all the time? The Watchers were just guessing at the potential threats to the community.

"You know what? It doesn't matter, because they're not going to see us. Right?" The answer was as much to calm her own rising nerves as it was to satisfy Tiko.

"Right."

"Good. So I need you to forget about all of those stars up there, watch where you're walking, and be super quiet until we make it back out here. Sometimes a true Zeduan Warrior has to rely on stealth instead of might."

Tiko puffed out his chest at those words. "I promise," he said as he touched a fist to his forehead. Kirra marveled at how much he looked like Taro in that moment. It was oddly comforting.

Her plan was to enter the copse of trees to shield themselves from view. Being out on these wide-open plains was starting to make her feel nervous, even if the tall grass did a good job of concealing them. Then they would slowly creep around the perimeter to see if they could discover anyone inside.

As it turned out, spying wasn't necessary. Because as soon as they got close to the mini forest, they could clearly hear the people within.

Kirra couldn't believe how noisy they were. Shouting and laughing and carrying on, even at this time of night. These people had broken the first rule of camping by scaring off any potential game animals. With the racket they were making, she'd be surprised if there were any birds left in the trees.

As they entered the forest and the light dimmed considerably, this little adventure started to seem like a very bad idea. She didn't want to take Tiko any closer, but she certainly couldn't leave him here on his own. What if she couldn't find him again in the dark on her way back out? All Kirra felt like doing, if she were being honest, was turning around and running all the way home.

She glanced down at Tiko, and as they listened to the boisterous sounds of the camp, the look on his face made it obvious he would be fully in favor of the sprinting-home plan. She grabbed his hand and took a step back out of the forest so that—

"Aaahhh!"

A scream cut through the rest of the camp noise. A primal sound of pain and fear.

Kirra felt a moment of water-kneed weakness before her resolve stiffened. She intended to do her part to protect Zedu no matter what. If these were indeed Takers and they posed a real threat, then her people had to be warned. Kirra would find answers, because Zedu deserved them.

"No! Please stop!"

The anguished pleas tore through the night air. Kirra took a deep breath. She would summon her courage and investigate, but she would not risk Tiko's safety any more than she already had. Scanning the woods around them, she picked out an unusual tree that would be easy to find again. It had a broad trunk and long branches that drooped in a dome-like shape, nearly touching the ground. Tiko would be safely concealed up there.

"Come here," she whispered. He complied without hesitation, clearly glad to have something to do other than stand there and listen to those horrible sounds coming from the camp. Kirra cupped both hands at her waist to form a foothold. "Step here," she whispered, "and grab that thick branch to pull yourself up."

When her little brother had clambered into the branches, Kirra pulled hard on the straps of her pack, cinching it tight to her body so that she'd be able to maneuver better. Tiko proved to be a natural at climbing trees, and soon they were some thirty feet above the ground. Kirra decided this would be more than high enough to hide her brother from anyone who might walk underneath.

She got close to his face. "You are going to stay here until

I return. Do *not* move from this spot, and do not make a noise. Understand?"

"But I want to help—"

Kirra raised a hand to cut him off. "I stayed true to my word. You are Outside. But now you will hold up your end of the bargain and do as I say. You *will* stay here until I get back."

Another scream tore the night apart to punctuate her command. Tiko gulped and nodded slowly.

Kirra leaned forward and kissed him on the forehead. Then she turned and scrambled along a limb, and leaped to a branch of a neighboring tree.

She remained high above the forest floor as she made her way toward the sounds of the camp, eyes accustomed to the dim light, hands and feet trained to find secure grips. Soon she was close enough to see the flickering light of campfires.

Kirra poked her head through a thick screen of leaves to find a limb on the next tree that could support her weight, and suddenly there was the camp spread out below her.

The first thing she noticed was the size of the group. There were a *lot* of people—mostly men, but a few women, too—sitting around the fire. No children that she could see. And nearby, tied to a tree, was a dog. Kirra's breathing became shallow. She knew dogs had keen senses and hoped it wouldn't detect her.

After Kirra had wrapped her mind around the huge

number of people in this camp, there was time to focus on the individual members. But she immediately regretted it. The word used by the uninvited storyteller back in Lukweii was disturbingly perfect: *monstrous.*

These intruders were so abnormally tall it looked like they had been stretched thin in some places. They were almost skeletal in their long arms and gaunt faces, but they had broad shoulders and big, powerful haunches. Their skin appeared leathery and tough, dimpled and a uniform ashy-gray color, like a rhinoceros's. Kirra wondered if they came from a desert environment, where that tough exterior would protect them from heat and sandstorms. Also, they each had a shock of bone-white hair, which she figured could have been bleached over time by prolonged exposure to the sun.

And their clothes. There were no animal hides or cloth robes. Instead, these people wore thick coverings of what looked like leather and some sort of shiny, hard material. They looked ready for battle—a real one.

Where could they possibly have come from?

The unsettling feeling deep in Kirra's chest that these people didn't belong here was about more than just their strange appearance. They seemed so clumsy as they lumbered around. They had somehow knocked down several small trees to clear a space for the camp, leaving logs and stumps for benches, and had recklessly trampled all the other vegetation nearby. From her bird's-eye vantage point, it looked to Kirra like an evil, lumbering giant from one of her father's scary stories had stamped an enormous foot in the middle of the forest and left this ragged clearing behind.

Kirra's stomach felt queasy—this went against everything she had been taught. Inside the volcano, each action one took could potentially affect others, so Zeduans behaved considerately. These Takers careened around as if nothing mattered.

Most unnerving of all was the source of those screams. A man, much smaller than the others and dressed to the waist in the robes of the Nafaluu, was tied to a tree. His feet were lashed to the trunk while his arms were stretched painfully high over his head and bound to branches above. People were occasionally punished for crimes in Zedu, but never like this. She wondered what horrible transgression the Nafaluu man had committed.

One of the Takers—taller than the rest, somehow, and thicker through the shoulders, with a bright red streak running through his white hair—stalked over to the tree and yelled into the criminal's cringing face. When he stopped shouting, Red Streak stepped back several paces, then flung one hand back over his shoulder. He was holding the handle of a leather strap, like something you might use to prod livestock, only this was much longer. He whipped his arm forward and the strap cut through the air. As the end of it snapped, it made a tremendous *crack* that cut through the noise of the camp and opened a bloody slash on the villager's chest. Kirra gasped, then covered her mouth. Tears sprang to her eyes and bile rose in her throat as she realized that the poor man already had several cuts across his bare torso, the fresh wounds glistening in the firelight. He screamed again and contorted his body against the tree trunk as if to get away, but there was no escape.

Kirra's first instinct was to run back to Tiko, but fear had rooted her in place. She didn't want to make any noise and risk being discovered by the man with the strap.

After stepping close to the villager again, Red Streak turned and addressed his group. He roared out a stream of unfamiliar words.

Kirra tilted her head and wrinkled her brow. During her travels with Taro, she had noticed that people from various villages had slightly different ways of talking, yet she was always able to understand them with no problem. This wasn't even close to the same thing.

After Red Streak shouted, the general tumult of the camp quieted considerably. He was clearly the leader. As the big man gestured broadly at the prisoner he had been tormenting, and everyone else in the encampment shifted positions or drew closer to observe the little scene, the meaning of his words was clear enough: The man from Nafaluu was ready to talk now.

Red Streak planted his boots in a wide stance in front

of the villager and crossed his unusually long arms over his chest. When he spoke again, it was in words that Kirra could make out, although in a rough, unfamiliar accent. The phrases came together haltingly, like when Tiko was just learning to talk.

"How many . . . number . . . people . . . in village?" Red Streak said, pointing in the general direction of Nafaluu. He then made punching gestures and mimed swinging some sort of weapon to emphasize his next words. "People . . . who . . . make war?"

The small man tied to the tree shook his head, eyes welling with tears. "Please. Nafaluu is a peaceful tribe. We have lived here for many years and had no problems with anyone. We only want—"

Crack! Red Streak snapped his cruel strap on the side of the tree, a clear reminder of what would happen again if his question wasn't answered.

The villager—a *captive*, not a criminal, Kirra realized—looked around the camp desperately but saw only sinister gray faces looking in his direction. Kirra tightened her grip on the tree limb as the man swallowed heavily. "All Nafaluu men are trained to fight."

Crack!

"Number," Red Streak growled. "Give me number."

The prisoner hung his head in misery and mumbled something inaudible.

Red Streak reared back again with the long leather strap, and Kirra winced, her whole body cringing in awful anticipation. But before he could deliver the punishing blow, another man emerged from the group. This new warrior, with a streak in his hair that brought to Kirra's mind the color of yellow thatching grass, stepped in between Red Streak and his captive.

The first man—the leader—yelled something at this newcomer. Yellowgrass put up both palms in a placating gesture and spoke to Red Streak in more of those words that Kirra could not begin to understand. Finally, Red Streak took a few grudging steps backward and made a sweeping gesture with his hands at the prisoner as if to say, *He's all yours.*

Yellowgrass approached the tree slowly and held a cup to the captive's lips for a few moments. The poor man gulped gratefully. Red Streak waved a hand dismissively and shook his head in disgust at this small gesture of kindness.

When Yellowgrass spoke, it was in the language of the Nafaluu. The words came slowly, but not nearly as forced as they had been with Red Streak.

"Please to answer questions," he said. With a quick but pointed glance at Red Streak, he continued. "I fear . . . more pain . . . if this you do not do." Yellowgrass sighed. "How many . . . fighting men . . . living in the village?" He bent close to the prisoner to hear his whispered answer.

Yellowgrass turned and addressed Red Streak in that strange language. The number must have been low, because upon hearing the report, the great warrior chuckled, a rumble from deep in his chest that got louder and louder until he threw back his head in full-throated laughter. His campmates raised their cups and joined him.

Finally Red Streak collected himself, spread his arms out, and patted the air with his palms to indicate the need for silence. When the crowd had simmered down, he turned his attention back to the interrogation. He spoke to Yellowgrass while looking and gesturing at the captive, clearly wanting another question to be asked.

Yellowgrass spoke to the prisoner, using mimed gestures to augment the limited language between the two. The man from Nafaluu merely shook his head, eyes wide in confusion and watery from terrified tears.

Kirra watched as Red Streak grabbed something belted around his waist. It was a long handle of some sort, wrapped in cloth and completely benign looking. But then Red Streak flicked his powerful wrist, and a long, sharp implement came shooting out with a hiss.

Kirra shivered, reminded of the dangerous retractable claws of the mighty lion in the stories that Taro had told her. This weapon was silver-toned, about four feet long and ending in a sharp point, like a very long cutting tool. But it was impossibly lean, clearly not crafted from stone. Whatever material it was made of shone and shimmered in the firelight. Red Streak slashed it this way and that, carving a pattern as the brutal instrument whistled through the air. Then he stepped forward, pushed Yellowgrass out of the way, and held it right under the prisoner's nose.

The Nafaluu man shook his head—carefully, so as to not come in contact with the sharp edge of the weapon in front of his eyes. "No," he said. "I have never seen anything like that."

More laughter erupted from the assembled crowd. Red Streak turned his head and barked another command at Yellowgrass.

"What do people of village . . . use?" the fair-haired man asked. "To . . . make war?"

The captive stared back with empty eyes. "We protect our village with spears."

Yellowgrass turned to Red Streak and mimed throwing a spear. The big warrior chuckled again and thrust his face close to the prisoner's. "Sticks." He spat the word out like it was a profanity. Then he extended a crooked gray talon of a finger. "You—fight—with—sticks." He poked the man's chest with each word.

Then, with two hands, Red Streak raised his silver instrument in the air, spun around, and, in one fluid motion, brought it crashing down on a low-hanging tree branch. Kirra gasped as it went through the wood with no resistance, leaving a neat little circle poking out of the trunk as the branch fell to the ground.

She shuddered. You didn't need a Storyteller's imagination to picture what would happen if these men brought such weapons into battle with the people of Nafaluu. It would not be a battle at all.

Kirra's whole body tensed as she felt the branch she was sitting on start to bounce. Oh no! One of their scouts? The thought flashed through her mind that if she were discovered, it would be bad for her, but much worse for Zedu. She whipped her head around, prepared to leap from the branch—

But it was just Tiko, slowly making his way toward her.

He must have followed her—at a distance. Kirra's relief lasted only half a moment. She did not want her little brother to see any of this. She held up a hand and mouthed, *Stop!* but it was too late. Tiko's eyes went wide as he surveyed the scene below them, a look of pure terror stealing across his face.

He pried his gaze away from the camp and shuffled along the branch, moving toward Kirra. He took one hand off the limb and reached for his sister. The gesture broke her heart—he looked just like he had when he was a frightened toddler seeking comfort.

The branch dipped sharply as he moved to her end. On instinct, Kirra's hand shot out and grabbed a limb above to stabilize herself.

The branch they were on cracked and broke in half. Kirra's stomach flopped, but she had the presence of mind to tighten her grip overhead and was left dangling in the air.

Tiko reached wildly for her but was not nearly quick enough. He plunged down into the middle of the camp.

7

KIRRA WATCHED IN HORROR as Tiko fell to the forest floor in a heap. Every head in camp snapped around to look at him.

Run! she desperately wanted to shout to him, but the word stuck in her throat.

Tiko didn't need any prompting. He bounced back up— thank the gods, nothing was broken—and dashed away into the darkest part of the forest.

But he was no match for this group of grown-ups, especially since they had clearly been trained for battle. The camp moved like an individual unit, fanning out to cut off his retreat, the warriors covering so much ground with each step of those long strides. Tiko cried out in surprise as he looked up and saw a towering wall of warriors in front of him. He nimbly switched directions and jumped over a log to light out for another part of the woods, but the wall shifted and blocked him again. While he managed to make it several yards away from the spot where he had first landed, Kirra watched in silent horror as her little brother was quickly surrounded.

What have I done? Kirra's first instinct was to let go of the branch and land down there with him, do whatever she could to protect her little brother.

But that would be foolish. What could she possibly do against Red Streak, with his cruel lash and clothing that seemed designed to protect him from a leopard attack? To say nothing of all his followers.

So she could only observe helplessly as Red Streak pushed his way through the crowd to where Tiko was cowering in terror. Hands on hips, the big man loomed over her brother. He reached down, grabbed Tiko by the scruff of his neck, and easily lifted him to his feet with one hand. Red Streak shouted some strange words into her little brother's face and then gestured overhead at the canopy of branches. "How many . . . in trees?"

Several of the warriors craned their necks to scan the branches above. Kirra was suddenly very glad that Tiko had been able to make it so far from the spot where he landed or they would all be looking directly up at her right now. Still, she knew she wasn't safe. Kirra carefully used both hands to hoist herself up and over the branch she was gripping. Then she slowly stood on trembling legs and stepped around to the other side of the thick trunk, concealing herself from the great circle of warriors. She peered around the trunk to take measure of the situation.

"Answer!" Red Streak thundered. He drew back his arm as if to deliver a backhanded slap to the small, trembling figure in front of him. Kirra covered her mouth to stifle a gasp as Tiko dropped to his knees and covered his head with both hands. This huge man could kill her little brother with one blow, no question.

Something broke inside of Kirra. She had to do something—*now*. But what?

She could feel the seconds racing past, her chance of helping Tiko before they tied him up, too (or worse, much worse), slipping away. Her chest felt squeezed almost shut, like she could hardly force in a breath.

Gripping the branch so tightly that the bark cut into her skin, Kirra had enough presence of mind left to try something that Paja had taught her. She closed her eyes, took a deep breath, and held it. She pictured her all-consuming panic as a great cloud and mentally compressed it until it was just a little ball in her chest. As she let out a long, controlled breath, she imagined the ball floating away on her breath and disappearing into the forest.

It worked. The fog lifted and she could think again. She snapped open her eyes and scanned the camp, looking for any kind of advantage. And because she was a bit calmer now, she was able to realize that the attention of the entire camp had shifted to Tiko. The Nafaluu prisoner, tied securely to the tree, had been forgotten for the time being.

That's when she got an idea. The use of force was not an option, obviously. She would have to do something sneakier. Having a plan—even a desperate one—helped to further calm her nerves.

It also helped when Yellowgrass made his way through the crowd and into the clearing where Red Streak was threatening her brother. He stepped past the huge warrior and helped Tiko get back up to his feet.

Sneering, Red Streak wielded that cruel silver weapon high over his head. But after a pointed look from Yellowgrass, he turned it upside down and jammed it into the ground close to the boy. The handle stretched above her brother's head.

Yellowgrass got down on one knee. "Are you . . . from village? Nafaluu?" The warrior pointed to the north.

Tiko shook his head.

Don't tell. Don't tell. Don't tell, Kirra pleaded silently.

"No? Hmm. Where you live? Where . . . your people?"

Kirra's heart stopped.

Tiko didn't even shake his head this time. He just set his jaw and glared back at the warriors in front of him.

Good boy, thought Kirra.

Red Streak grunted in frustration and pushed Yellowgrass out of the way. "Answer. Now. How many . . . in forest?" The command came out almost conversationally, hardly more than a whisper, but Kirra could hear the menace behind it, as sharp as the weapon that was mere inches from Tiko's face.

Her brother just silently stood his ground.

At this show of defiance, Red Streak glared at Yellowgrass and reached for his weapon, but the fair-haired warrior stepped closer to Tiko. "Please . . . little one . . . talk to us."

The two warriors continued their interrogation, but Kirra was no longer watching. The window for her being able to be useful was rapidly closing. Racing along the branch, she leaped to a neighboring tree, climbed through the thick limbs there, and jumped to the next tree. In this way, she circled over the heads of the warriors below, making her way toward the captive.

When she reached his tree, she scrambled down the back of it to the ropes that were binding his arms. Wrapping her legs around the trunk, she glanced quickly at the gathering of warriors to make certain Tiko was still unhurt and holding their attention, then she whispered to the prisoner.

"Hey! Up here!"

Startled, the poor man from Nafaluu twisted his neck to look at her. Kirra put a finger over her lips to make sure he didn't cry out. When he had recovered from the shock of seeing a young girl appear from the dark canopy of the forest, she went on. "If I free you, will you do a favor for me?"

The man nodded enthusiastically, eyes wide.

Kirra fished out her cutting stone and furiously went to work on the rope that held his right arm above his head. She continued to whisper as she sawed. "As soon as you can, start running to your village. Warn them." The man wriggled his wrist free as the rope fell. Kirra started in on the bonds lashing his other hand to the tree. "But here is the favor: Count to a hundred as you run. When you reach the end, stop in your tracks, scream as loud as you can, and then take off running again. Will you do this?" The man gulped but silently nodded.

Kirra released both of his hands and then dropped to the ground to work on freeing his left ankle. The man stooped over to untie the right. As her cutting stone ate away at the thick rope, she kept one eye trained on the group of men surrounding Tiko.

Oh, dear gods, no.

Red Streak was now screaming at Tiko. But that wasn't what suddenly had her heart in an icy grip.

It was Yellowgrass. His gray head was turned, and he was looking directly at her.

There was no use running, nothing she could do. So she redoubled her efforts and sawed as quickly as she could.

Then suddenly the man was free.

And when she looked back at the group . . . what was happening? Yellowgrass had not raised the alarm. He had turned his attention back to Red Streak and her little brother. But she knew he had seen her. She would have staked her life on it.

The Nafaluu prisoner jolted her out of her jumbled thoughts. "Oh, thank you. May the gods bless you. I must—"

"Go," Kirra whispered fiercely, shoving him in the direction of his village. "Just remember our deal."

The man nodded once and stealthily took off through the forest.

There was no time for his words of thanks. Besides, Kirra knew that she didn't really deserve them, anyway. She had untied the man more for Tiko's sake than his own.

Kirra looped a coil of rope over her shoulder and scurried her way up the tree trunk again, counting in her head.

Fifteen . . . sixteen . . . seventeen . . .

"Show us you are . . . big warrior." Below her, Red Streak was trying a new tactic with her brother. The man grabbed the handle of his weapon and pulled it out of the dirt. He swung it with ease over Tiko's head, the boy trying to be brave and stand still as the silver blade whistled through the night air, just barely missing him. Yellowgrass had backed up to a safe distance but was keeping a steady eye on the proceedings. And he still had not raised the alarm.

Twenty-four . . . twenty-five . . . twenty-six . . .

Kirra scooched across a thick tree branch, trying to balance her desperate need for haste with an even greater need to be silent.

Red Streak stopped slashing the air with his weapon. He brought it down and, carefully holding the blade with both hands, presented it to Tiko handle-first with a formal bow.

"You try, big warrior."

Forty-one . . . forty-two . . . forty-three . . .

Tiko looked warily at Red Streak, unmoving, until the big man thumped him in the chest with the handle. "You . . . hear me," he growled.

Tiko grabbed it with both hands, but as soon as Red Streak let go of the blade, the weapon fell to the dirt. Tiko staggered to his knees.

Raucous laughter erupted from Red Streak's platoon of fighters. But Tiko planted the point in the dirt again, climbed hand over hand along the weapon's handle to get back up, placed his feet apart, braced himself, and slowly raised the weapon.

Fifty-nine . . . sixty . . . sixty-one . . .

Kirra inched across a limb, so focused on being quiet that she was holding her breath. She maneuvered into position directly above Red Streak and her brother. Moving as quickly as she dared, she looped one end of the rope around the branch and fastened it with a knot that Paja had taught her.

Below, Tiko grunted, shifting his hips and shoulders as he swung the weapon at Red Streak with all of his might. The hulking man took a surprised step back but easily got a thick leather boot up in time to kick the heavy instrument out of Tiko's hands. Yellowgrass bent and picked up the weapon.

Kirra positioned the rope as carefully as she could. There would only be one shot at pulling this off.

Eighty-three . . . eighty-four . . . eighty-five . . .

"Aaahhh!" There was a scream in the distance. But this one was defiant, not pained. That guy must have been a fast counter.

Every head in the camp, including Red Streak's, snapped toward the source of the noise. At that exact moment, Kirra let the rope fall. It dangled just in front of Tiko's face. A perfect drop.

Tiko's head craned up at the rope, and Kirra made frantic gestures for him to grab it.

There wouldn't have been enough time for Tiko to climb—he would have been noticed and plucked off the rope immediately—had Yellowgrass not yelled and pointed in the direction of the scream. He rallied everyone, including Red Streak, to pursue the escaped prisoner.

"Hurry!" Kirra hissed fiercely as Tiko took the rope with both hands, wrapped his knees around it, and started clambering up.

Red Streak was a few yards away when he automatically reached for his weapon. Realizing he'd left it behind, he turned back to his little spy and—

"Arrgghh!" There was a cry of surprised rage as the big warrior spotted Tiko halfway up the rope. He dashed over, and Kirra saw that Tiko wasn't going to make it. He wasn't high enough.

She hooked her knees around the tree branch and let herself fall upside down, her hands reaching for Tiko as her hair hung in her face, obscuring her view and making the panic flood back into her mind.

Red Streak jumped up, his fingers grasping at Tiko's foot.

Tiko let go of the rope and lunged for Kirra's hands, grabbing them tightly. He latched on, and the momentum sent him sailing through the air, his sister's arms acting as a swing. Kirra gripped the tree with the back of her knees, wincing in pain as her legs twisted around the branch and the rough bark rubbed patches of skin right off.

Tiko slammed into another branch, let go of Kirra's hands, and hooked his armpits over the limb. He was out of reach, at least for the moment.

Red Streak had missed Tiko's foot, but he grabbed the rope and began to hoist himself up, his boots climbing the trunk. Kirra, still dangling upside down and swinging back in his direction, was only a few feet away from his powerful hands.

But she heard the branch start to crack under his weight. As she swung backward, she flailed out with her hands and grasped at another limb.

Taking one arm off the rope, Red Streak lunged for Kirra. He came mere inches from reaching her leg . . . and the branch broke. Kirra, her heart racing, watched as Red Streak's eyes went wide. He seemed to hang suspended in the air before he dropped and crashed to the forest floor, landing squarely on his back.

For an agonizing moment, Red Streak and Kirra were locked in a death gaze. She could feel anger radiating from him like heat waves off a desert rock.

Red Streak tried to summon his clan, but the wind had been knocked out of him. Kirra reacted quickly. She hopped up on the limb, raced over to Tiko, grabbed him by the hand, and pulled him higher up the tree until they were totally concealed by the foliage.

Red Streak got his voice back and started shouting for his warriors to help. Or he may have been cursing—Kirra had no way of knowing.

A few men ran back and tried to scramble up into the trees after them, but their bulky clothing and the awkward, heavy weapons still belted to their waists made climbing difficult. Plus, even with their long limbs, they looked awkward and unfamiliar with climbing—Kirra knew that there were very few trees in the desert. She felt a quick burst of confidence that she and Tiko, being much lighter and more nimble, had the advantage.

"Come with me," she whispered fiercely, yanking her brother along a thick and sturdy branch. He followed without a word.

Kirra had learned from her experiences in Outside woods that she could travel more quickly above the forest floor than people could on the ground, where they would run into brush, logs, swampy patches, and other obstacles.

So they fled through the middle of the trees, the horrible sounds of the camp fading behind them.

As they neared the plains, the noise dwindling to nothing, Kirra finally felt that they could stop for a moment. She turned to Tiko and asked breathlessly, "Why did you come to me when I told you not to?"

Tiko's lip trembled as he looked at her with big, moist eyes. "I heard bad noises," he said. "And I wanted to protect you."

Kirra couldn't be angry with him for that. "You truly are a birdbrain. But I love you."

They made their way through one last screen of trees and finally spotted the ocean of wild grass that stood between them and their home. "Now, follow me. We need to run faster and farther than we've ever run before."

They dropped from branch to branch until they were back on the ground. Then they entered the plains in the tallest patch of grass they could find, and disappeared into the night.

BY GOD, THE GIRL WAS FAST.

Cobar the Red had not been forced to run this far in a long time. He shook his head in disgust as he pounded through the tall grass in heavy boots he wasn't accustomed to. Back home, there were horses when someone needed to cover this kind of distance.

It was a good thing this land was so rich with resources. Definitely made the whole venture worth it, no question. But still, he missed having a horse.

At least he had his hound. He wouldn't have been able to

track these kids otherwise, because they did not slow, or tire. The dog strained at his leash, practically dragging him right across the plains. The beast might be simple, but at least it was loyal. Could he say the same for Dekker, his so-called right-hand man? That one seemed to be going soft on these natives.

Strange that the kids were running in the opposite direction of the village. Were they confused? Or were they trying to throw him off track? He had to admit they were wily little devils, freeing his captive when his back was turned. . . .

Now they were making a beeline straight for the dormant volcano. Were they just running in blind panic? Every native in every village for miles around was as superstitious as hellfire about that place. Thought it could erupt at any time and kept a healthy distance always.

Cobar pulled sharply on the leash before his dog could break through the overgrown grass into the open ground at the base of the volcano. He squatted, stroking the slavering beast with his long gray fingers and talking soothingly to keep it quiet. Then he peeked his head through the screen of grass.

He watched for a bit, tracking the children as they made their way up the steep and craggy mountain. He couldn't believe how fast they were still moving after all that climbing and running. And then, in a blink, they were gone. One moment they were winding through a series of switchbacks, and the next moment they couldn't be seen. Didn't make sense.

Unless . . .

Cobar scratched his leathery chin. The two little ones were well fed, that much was certain, with clothing that—primitive though it might have been—was made with some skill. These were no feral strays. These kids belonged to a community.

He stared up at the crater for several minutes, bright eyes piercing through the darkness. He shook his head slowly. It couldn't be, could it? But really, there was no other answer.

He chuckled to himself. The dog turned to look at him and started to whimper.

Cobar would never have guessed that any of these natives were clever enough. But they had made a nest within the crater walls. . . . Hidden away like that, there was no telling what kind of paradise might be inside. He let his eyes drift over the mountain. This was a much bigger operation than that little village by the waterfall. That place didn't seem worth the trouble now.

He spent a long time marking the spot where the kids had disappeared, memorizing the identifying features of the landscape that would lead him right back to the doorstep.

First he would go back and fetch some help, soldiers he could count on. He was going to need it, because there might be all manner of treasure stashed away in that volcano.

Cobar the Red couldn't wait to find out.

8

WHEN KIRRA WOKE UP, bruised and tender all over from the events of the previous night, her secret was a physical presence in the bedroom. It sat on her chest like a pile of stones, making it difficult to breathe. It whispered in her ear about what a horrible daughter and sister she had been to her family, to her tribe, to all Zedu. She couldn't escape it— everywhere she looked, it was staring her right in the face.

She didn't even have to debate herself. It was obvious what she had to do. Her mother and father had to know, right away, about the Takers and what had happened. Yes, there would be a punishment unlike anything she had ever endured. Yes, her parents' disappointment would be so deep they probably wouldn't talk to her for years and years. And yes—this was the worst part—she might not be allowed to go Outside ever again.

But Zedu had to be protected. So she pushed herself painfully out of bed, trudged through the hut, and made her way to the back porch.

However, the big chair where her mother sat every morning to go over Council notes was empty. Same with the courtyard—the shared communal space was free of the usual morning bustle. Making her way quickly around to the front of the hut, Kirra blinked and looked out at the great ring of terraces that circled the inside of their volcano home. At different points of the day, as the sun moved through the heavens, the various sections of the community received direct light that filtered in through the narrow opening at the top of the volcano. You could always tell what time it was by which terrace was lit up. And if Kirra could trust her senses, it looked like she had slept well past noon.

She raced back into the hut and looked everywhere, but neither of her parents was home. Next she went into Tiko's quarters and found her little brother still snoring heavily. She thought about whether or not to wake him up and finally decided she couldn't risk him talking to her parents before she did. The secret would simply be too big for him, and she was going to need to manage the way in which they got this particular message.

Kirra sat on her brother's mattress and placed a hand on his arm. Immediately, Tiko cried out in terror and bolted upright in bed, eyes wild.

Her heart sank. This was all her fault. By taking her brother Outside, Kirra had exposed him to something that would continue to haunt him for the rest of his life. How could she have been so stupid? So selfish?

"Shhh. It's okay, Tiko. It's just me. It's okay." She patted him on the arm to calm him down. "We're home. We're safe."

Tiko took a deep breath and slowly relaxed. The two siblings sat that way for several moments, collecting themselves and sinking into the fact that they had, indeed, made it back within the protecting walls of Zedu.

"What are we going to do, Kirra?" Tiko whispered.

"*You* don't have to do anything, Tiko. *I* will tell Paja and Maja what happened." He nodded as she spoke soothingly. "And then they will go to the Council and discuss what to do to protect Zedu from those awful people. Our part is over—it should have never even started. This problem is one for the grown-ups, understand?"

"But there were so many of them, Kirra. And they were so big, and they looked so . . . so . . ." Tiko was staring into the middle distance, eyes unfocused, clearly reliving the events of the previous night and struggling to describe the monstrous Takers. "Those weapons—so terrible. Never seen anything like it. And that horrible leader, with the—"

"Shh." Kirra grabbed her little brother and held him close when the tears started leaking out of his eyes. "I know it was scary. I know. I was scared, too." She ran her hand along his back like their mother used to do when they were little. "But we are home now. Safe. No one knows Zedu is here. It's been that way for many, many generations." These were her father's words, and as she said them, they comforted her as well as her brother.

Tiko let out a long breath, relieved. He pulled back from his sister and wiped at his eyes. "Okay, but who are they? And how did you know they would be there? And why didn't Paja—"

Kirra held up a hand, cutting him off. "None of that matters right now. First I need to find him and tell everything we know."

"But I can—"

"I know you want to help. For now, though, I just need you to lie low until I can get to him. Maybe take the day away from our terrace and play with your friends. Try to forget about it for a few hours, if you can. Come back at dinner and I should have it all sorted out."

After a few moments of contemplation, Tiko gave her a sidelong glance. "We're going to be in trouble, aren't we?"

"Oh, yes."

"Big trouble?"

"The biggest."

Tiko sighed. "Okay, then. I guess it's a good idea for me to go play with Derain and Miki. Might be the last time I see them for a while."

Kirra managed a half smile. "Probably a good plan."

Tiko climbed out from underneath his covers and started to get dressed. Kirra rose to leave the room, then stopped in the doorway.

"Tiko?"

"Yeah?"

"I'm proud of you. You know, for the way you handled yourself last night. Even better than a Zeduan Warrior, if there were such a thing."

Tiko beamed. "Thanks, Kirra."

She waved good-bye and made her way down the front steps and across the terrace. It would have been easier to find her mother—Kirra knew she would be in the Council chambers—but she wanted to talk to Taro first. Having spent so much time Outside, he might be slightly more understanding about what she had done. And besides, even though she would never admit it out loud, she had a special bond with her father that made him easier to approach than her mom.

The problem was, Taro could be anywhere. Part of his

job was to roam widely throughout the interior of the volcano, staying up on current events and collecting bits of information that he would weave together in his stories of Zedu and her people. He could rarely be found in the same spot two days in a row, which was one of the reasons that Kirra wanted to be a Storyteller. She couldn't imagine having to go to the same place every day for work.

So she set out to wander along the terraces, asking after him—Farmers, Bakers, Couriers, Herders—but no one had seen her father. The longer she had to keep her dark revelation to herself, the heavier it became to carry.

After several hours—the fading light falling on the eastern terraces signaling an imminent sunset—she gave up looking for Taro. He could be anywhere.

So she would have to approach her mother first. She took a deep breath, tried to summon some courage, and headed back in the direction of the Council chambers. When Kirra arrived, Djiahna was just walking out. She looked tired.

"Oh, hello, sweetheart. What brings you this way?"

"I need to talk to you."

"Perfect. We'll walk home together." Djiahna linked her arm with her daughter's. "I couldn't wake you this morning! Did you two have a wild night while the grown-ups worked on the festival?"

Kirra swallowed hard as her stomach flipped, but she

could tell from Djiahna's quick smile that she was just making a joke. It made Kirra's heart ache to see such a trusting and loving look on her mother's face. This was going to be even more difficult than she'd been dreading it would be.

"Do . . . do you know when Paja will be coming home? I need to speak with both of you."

Djiahna's eyebrows scrunched up. "What's wrong, precious one?"

Kirra looked down at the ground as they walked. "It will be easier to tell you both at the same time," she mumbled.

Djiahna stopped walking and let go of Kirra's arm. "Your father had to leave this morning."

"I know, I've been looking all over for him. When will he be back?"

Maja hesitated before answering, and cleared her throat. "I'm not quite sure. He didn't just go to another terrace this time. He had to . . . Kirra, he had to go Outside again."

Kirra's head snapped up. "What?" *So soon?* she thought. *We just got back yesterday! And he never goes Outside without me anymore.* "Why?"

"I'm afraid I cannot discuss that with you."

"But I'm a Helper now! This is important, and I'm supposed to know what—"

Djiahna put her hand up. "It's official Council business. You know I'm forbidden to share any details with you."

Kirra's head spun. It had to be connected to what she'd overheard them talking about yesterday. Nothing else would take him away from home so soon.

She inhaled deeply. There was no more time for secrets, or hesitation. A horrifying image rose up in her mind of Taro lashed to a tree trunk. She could *not* let Paja be discovered by Red Streak and the rest of his awful soldiers, no matter what might happen to her afterward. "When did he leave?"

"He was helping me with Council matters for most of the day, so he ended up leaving Zedu about an hour ago, but I don't see what that has to do with—"

An hour! "At least tell me this, I beg you—did he go to Nafaluu? To see what's happening there, or to warn them, maybe?"

Djiahna sputtered and didn't reply right away, but the look on her mother's face—shock and confusion mixed with the beginning of anger—was all the answer Kirra needed.

She turned and raced to the edge of the terrace, jumped off to land in the cushion of leaves and moss, then popped right back up and kept running.

Maja cried out behind her, but Kirra was not worried about pursuit. Even on sore and tired legs she knew she was faster.

And she would need every last bit of that speed. *He left an hour ago!* she thought. If Taro had gone directly to the village, he could nearly be there by now.

The activities on each terrace passed by in a blur, friends and extended family members calling out unanswered greetings. Kirra raced on, the pain in her legs forgotten, everything forgotten except the need to get Outside and find Paja before something terrible happened to him.

She finally arrived at the closest exit tunnel. Her friend, the Watcher's Helper Tatuu, sat with her back against the stone wall, eating a bowl of vegetables.

"Tatuu!" Kirra was panting. "You must help me. Where is your Watcher? In the tunnel?"

Tatuu nodded but regarded her friend warily. "Kirra, why are you so—?"

"I need you to distract him. Get him away from the exit for just a minute so I can sneak Outside."

Tatuu's eyes went wide. "But your father already left, and he said—"

"It doesn't matter. I'm going alone. Please. Help me. Now." Kirra hopped from one foot to the other impatiently.

"*Alone?*" Tatuu glanced uneasily at the entrance to the tunnel. "But, Kirra, you know I can't. I could lose my position as—"

Kirra turned and dashed away from her friend. There was no time to argue. With each passing second Paja could be in more danger. Rules no longer applied.

She stormed into the tunnel and barreled through its twists and turns. At the end of the passageway, the official

Watcher knelt at the exit with his back to her, eyes trained on the surrounding landscape just beyond the volcano's wall.

Kirra knocked into him as she ran past. "Hey!" he yelled. Dashing into the rapidly dimming light of dusk on the Outside, she could hear footsteps pounding the earth behind her, but she wasn't worried about that, either. For one thing, she had never been faster. She doubted any grown-up could catch her under normal circumstances, and panic was giving her supernatural speed and energy. And for another thing, there seemed to be an invisible barrier around Zedu for anyone who was not a traveling Storyteller. The Watcher would soon grow very uncomfortable Outside, and he would go back and report her rather than follow her into the unknown.

Who cares? Kirra thought. *Let him report me. The only thing that matters is getting Paja home safely.*

9

KIRRA STUMBLED DOWN the rough volcano wall, falling and skinning her knee. But she popped right back up again. She ran through the searing pain of a stitch in her side, ignored the sharp stones she stepped on and her parched throat that cried out for water. Soon it was so dark she could hardly see where she was placing her next footstep. Still, she ran.

Nearing the bottom of the wall, she encountered a great rocky ridge and hurriedly picked her way along its length. On the other side would be the plains, and then it would be a dead sprint all the way to Nafaluu. She would somehow—

"Paja?!"

Was this a vision created out of pure desperation? Taro, dashing around the side of the ridge in disheveled robes?

She stood frozen to the spot, squinting through the murky twilight as the moon rose to replace the sun. The vision ran right up to her, dropped to one knee, and grabbed her fiercely by the shoulders. This was all happening so quickly she couldn't tell what was real. The rough way his fingers dug into her flesh told her this was no hallucination, but she simply couldn't believe the expression on her father's face, his eyes so wild it seemed as if they were staring right through her.

"Kirra! What are you doing out here?"

"I . . . I didn't . . ."

"There's no time!" He cupped her face with both of his hands. "They are nearly here. I don't know how, but they found out about Zedu. They know where we live!"

The inside of Kirra's belly went cold.

"Listen to me." He glanced frantically over his shoulder, then back at Kirra. "You need to hide, and when it is safe, you must go to Lukweii. Tell the leader of their tribe who you are and what you have seen. Ask them to shelter you until it is safe to return." Another desperate look behind them. "*If* it is ever safe to return."

"Paja, I don't want—"

Taro pulled her close, planted a rough kiss on her cheek,

then embraced her, squeezing so hard that it hurt. "I love you, Kirra," he whispered fiercely into her ear. "Never forget it."

A great shout rose from the other side of the ridge, answered by more voices roaring in unison. Taro pulled back, listening, his eyes going even wider. Kirra felt like she was stuck in a terrible dream. None of this seemed like it could be happening, not really, especially not this fast.

"Listen carefully, Kirra." Taro motioned to a small, protected area underneath a rocky overhang. He took her by the shoulders and pushed her down, first on her knees and then over onto her side. Limp from exhaustion and terror, she curled up into a ball like a scared armadillo. He shoved her underneath the outcropping of stone.

"But, Paja, I—"

"Please, Kirra." His voice was thick. Peeking out, she saw something she had never seen before: Her father was crying. Somehow that single detail cut through everything else that was happening, the tears streaming down Taro's face making all of this horribly real. He uprooted some brush and pressed it under the lip of rock, covering her. "I must go. I have to try and warn the others. Don't move until it's safe. I love you. I'm so sorry. I'm so sorry I couldn't do more to protect you, my sweet one."

Then he turned and raced away, climbing the side of the volcano in long, loping strides.

Kirra whimpered and reached out for him, but she froze when she heard the strange men shouting again, closer this time. She pulled her arm back under the ledge. In another moment, a group of tall warriors from the camp ran around the ridge, lighting up the night sky with flaming torches. The group blasted right past her, sending a cloud of dust into her hiding place. She squeezed her eyes shut, tasting dirt that threatened to choke her. By the gods, they covered so much ground in those great, bounding strides. How would her father ever have a chance to warn the people of Zedu?

Some long minutes later, when the entire procession had passed and she was able to peel open her eyes, she watched through the leaves in horror as her nightmare came true—her father disappeared into the volcano, but with the entire group of Red Streak's men right on his heels. They all had those terrible shiny blades in their hands, pointed at the sky, the light from their flames winking off the cruel, sharpened tips. A few of them dashed in the tunnel; the others waited outside the entrance. Just a few minutes later, the first warriors returned and waved in the rest. The assembly—it looked like an even bigger group than she had seen in the woods, if that were possible—stormed into the same entrance she and Tiko had snuck back through last night, squeezing those long gray bodies and all of that armor and weaponry through the crack in Zedu's volcano wall.

All the air left Kirra in a dizzying rush.

Had the Takers followed her and Tiko as they raced across the plains toward home? Oh, dear gods, that was the only possible explanation.

Kirra went light-headed as she couldn't suck in a desperately needed breath. Zedu had lived peacefully behind the protective walls of the volcano for generation upon generation, and after Kirra's first unauthorized trip Outside, they were overrun within the space of a single day.

Zedu was being seen by Outsider eyes for the first time at this very moment. Unthinkable, yet it was happening, and she was to blame.

The interior of the volcano was being met with those cruel weapons and open flames, while she was out here. No one was safe . . . Paja . . . Maja . . . little Tiko . . . all her friends . . . and it was entirely her fault.

That's when Kirra's mind gave out and the world went dark.

When she came to, it was many hours later. The sun was directly overhead, the air hot and still.

She was so stiff she could barely move. Her arms and legs were scratched up from the brush, she itched all over, and grit coated her tongue. As she took inventory of her body, her mind slowly recalled where she was . . . and why. Overwhelmed with fear, dread, and guilt, she was unable to muster the energy to fix any of her minor discomforts. A feeling settled into her chest so strongly she knew it would always be there from this point on: She deserved to be miserable. Now and forever.

She lay there, listless, until the sky darkened again, the moon rose slowly over the volcano, and the air became so cold she couldn't stop shivering.

Occasionally warriors marched back and forth past her hiding spot. Kirra squeezed her eyes shut. She clapped her hands over her ears, but still the relentless sound of their pounding boots came.

When the sun rose again, Kirra's mouth was so dry that it hurt to move her tongue. An idea drifted in, slipped under the ledge of rock, and wormed its way into her head: If she didn't get out soon and get some water, she was going to die here.

Kirra closed her eyes tightly again and didn't move, giving herself over to fate.

The sound of rain falling on the rocks outside woke Kirra. In all the confusion of the last few days, she had missed the telltale signs of an incoming monsoon, but it was here now. The water fell in great sheets.

Acting more on deep-seated instinct than a conscious will to survive, Kirra stuck her hand out from under the ledge, let the rain wet her fingers, and pulled them back to suck on them.

Her throat was so dry and constricted that at first it felt like she was swallowing sand. But as she slowly collected more fresh rainwater, her mouth loosened up and she gained a bit of strength.

She eventually crawled into the open, leaving herself completely exposed. But what of it? True, one of the warriors could spot her, but that would only speed up what needed to happen. Kirra should not be allowed to live.

She stood there in the downpour, tears mixing with the rain streaming down her face, and looked up at the hidden entrance to the volcano. But there was no one about. Were all the Takers inside now, using everything the Zeduans had built to keep themselves dry and warm and fed?

How could she have lost her entire world so quickly?

And how could it . . . oh, gods, how could it possibly have been all her fault? She'd only wanted to help. She'd wanted to serve Zedu and help her father and use stories to teach and protect her people. And now Zedu and Paja and all of his stories . . .

She felt dizzy and sick to her stomach, but she had to

know what was happening inside. What she had caused to happen.

Kirra knew better than to try going through the nearby entrance. The warriors would have manned it, first thing.

So instead she summoned a reserve of energy she didn't think she possessed and willed her shaking legs to climb to the very top of the volcano.

When she arrived, Kirra lifted her gaze from the ground to find something straight out of one of her father's stories—smoke. Not the gentle, continuous puffs the Calla twins produced to create the illusion that the volcano was about to erupt. Instead, big, dark, ominous clouds of choking smoke were billowing from the top of the crater.

When she made it to the rim she collapsed, her cheek pressed against the dirt. She grabbed the lip of the crater and pulled herself forward on her belly, trying to find a break in the smoke where she could breathe.

As her eyes adjusted and she was able to peer down into the only place she had ever called home, she was thankful for all that smoke.

The hazy picture that emerged was horrifying enough. Nearly every structure in the community was a heap of charred wood and ash. There was no sign of life inside.

The fire demons had turned out to be real, after all.

She pushed herself away, choking and gagging, staggered

away from the crater, and stumbled back down the volcano wall.

Her mind tried to find explanations for what she had seen. It didn't work.

As she half walked, half slid down the rain-slicked mountain, she tried to turn her mind off entirely, but that didn't work, either. Paja had told her to go back to Lukweii for sanctuary. She didn't deserve that. Besides, one of the Takers would probably follow her, and she would lead him right to a fresh village for the slaughter. That was her legacy now. Instead of spreading stories, she spread destruction.

She would not go to Lukweii, or Nafaluu, or any place where there were people trying to enjoy their lives.

Her exhausted and cramped legs plodded on until she had walked straight off the volcano. She waded through tall grass and thorny bushes and puddles and under trees until finally she was standing on the banks of the great river. The ledge she was on overlooked the rushing water some ten or so feet below. But this downpour was working quickly. She could see the swollen river rising to meet her. The deluge was creating tangles of whitewater, swift eddies, and boiling whirlpools. If someone were to fall in, they would have no chance. Their body would be spun around and dragged under and tossed about until the life was sucked out of them. They would be gone.

And all their terrible memories would be gone with them.

Perhaps Kirra's feet dislodged some rocks, or maybe the strong rain had made the ledge unstable. In any case, the ground slid underneath her.

Kirra fell into the river and was swept away from everything she had ever known.

SHE WAS FREEZING. *Chill had seeped into her body so completely that it felt like an essential part of her.*

She went where the current took her. There was no other choice. She was spun this way and that, sucked under the water only to be spit out above the surface several suffocating moments later. Her body bounced off logs and rocks as if it were a piece of trash that had been dumped into the current. If she weren't numb with cold, she would have felt the pain much more keenly.

Darkness started creeping in around the edges of her vision. Her physical numbness was so complete it no longer fazed her when freezing whitewater splashed over her face. Her emotional numbness was so complete she didn't care if she ever made it out of here.

Time became meaningless. She had always been here. The darkness increased, limiting her sight. The numbness continued to seep in until she couldn't feel anything anymore.

Until the hand. Warm and strong, it slipped into hers. It pulled her, gave her direction. Reminded her there were other things besides cold and wet and pain. That hand became her entire world.

Then there was total blackness.

When she regained the tiniest part of herself, she found the strength to open her eyes. She saw a boy's face, unfamiliar but kind.

He looked down at her. His mouth moved. Several moments later the voice came to her, muffled and distorted, as if she were still underwater. Maybe she was.

"You're going to be okay."

No, she wanted to tell him, I'm not. But she couldn't say anything. Her lips didn't feel right.

She wasn't touching the ground. At first, she thought she might be floating, but then she understood that this boy was carrying her. As a canopy of branches rushed by overhead, she realized she was in a forest.

"What's your name?" the boy asked her.

Kirra, *she answered in her head. Was that still her name? Did you actually have a name if everyone who knew it was gone?*

"You're going to be okay," *he said again.*

Then they were standing at the base of a tree, and the boy was craning his neck to look up, yelling for help.

And then it was black again.

Part Two
The Tree Folk

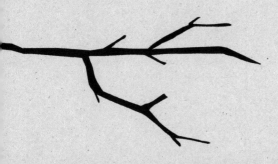

10

ANY MEMBER OF THE Tree Folk could leave the community and wander about the surrounding lands whenever they wanted. But fourteen-year-old Kirra rarely did.

Instead, it was her preference to stay safely inside the hut, doing daily chores such as preparing food or mending clothes. She had to admit, though, that *safe* was a relative term when the hut was located more than two hundred dizzying feet above the ground.

Even after four years of living in it, Kirra still marveled at the structure. The dwelling had been built in a circle around the top of a great tree. The trunk rose through a hole in the middle of the floor in the main living room and disappeared through the roof. Up this high, the trunk was much thinner than it was at the forest floor far below, but it was still thick enough to provide sturdy support for the hut and the four people who lived there.

Underneath the wooden platform that served as the floor hung a series of sleeping hammocks, accessible through trapdoors. Branches had been cleared to allow room for the living space, where the family kept their possessions and shared meals.

A stone fire pit for cooking had been constructed well away from the tree trunk, underneath a hole in the roof that let smoke escape. Many layers of smooth river rocks formed the base. You had to be extremely careful with fire when you lived at the top of a towering tree. One stray spark could—

Kirra shook her head to make that thought go away. Fire was definitely one of her Memory Traps.

A Memory Trap could suck her in like a whirlpool and force her to spin backward. Back to Before. And then her mind, dragging her heart along with it, would end up in a very bad place.

It had happened often when she first arrived. Almost everything had been a Memory Trap then, and whenever she'd allowed herself to dwell on certain things, she would inevitably spiral downward. Then she'd spend several days in a row not talking and hardly moving. She knew it had frightened and disturbed the people who had taken her in. And she didn't want that. They'd been very kind to her.

Kirra had become quite adept at avoiding these mental pitfalls. At first, it had felt like physically pushing the bad thoughts away against their will, cramming them into too-small boxes and shoving them back into the deep storage areas of her brain. But now she could do it almost automatically, avoid a looming Memory Trap as if she were merely sidestepping an ankle-twisting hole while walking in the woods.

When the bad thoughts about fire threatened to pop up, she shifted her attention to the pot of stew bubbling over the flames. It was time to dip a wooden ladle into the soupy mixture of mushrooms, greens, and meat and taste-test it. But Kirra made a face after one slurp. She definitely needed to add salt before the others returned.

She stood and ran a finger along the shelf of kitchen goods, then pursed her lips and blew out a frustrated breath. The salt bowl was nearly empty. Again. She was pretty sure it was Luwan's turn to refill it, but he was out having fun somewhere in the forest. Again.

Kirra sighed. It would take over half an hour to make her way to the salt caverns. Maybe forty-five minutes. Definitely more than an hour round-trip. Dinner would be late.

Hmm. Maybe she could serve the stew as is? She grabbed

the ladle, took another tentative sip, and . . . ugh. No. Salt was a necessity.

Kirra shook her head slowly. Her first instinct was to seek out a neighbor and ask if she could borrow some, bringing along a small gift of thanks in return. That made more sense than trekking all the way to the caverns. In fact, that's certainly what she would have done back in the old days when—

No, no. Nope. Stop. Anything she would have done in the old days was a Memory Trap, even something as simple as visiting a neighbor. No sense taking even another moment to ponder it.

Besides, that was not how things were done here. Tree families mostly kept to themselves. You were aware of and might become acquainted with the people who lived in the closest surrounding trees, but not in any real or intimate way. You couldn't even see them most of the time, since the individual homes were so well hidden. There was very little sharing of resources; people were expected to fend for themselves. The community structure did not lend itself to casually dropping by and asking if you could borrow some salt.

Instead, she grabbed the large pouch from the hook, looped it around her shoulders so it rested on her back, and prepared for her journey.

She poured a gourd full of water over the flames and the fire disappeared with an angry hiss and a great poof of steam. It would be a pain to get it going again to reheat the stew, but there were no unattended fires when you lived in the treetops.

Taking a deep breath, she walked out the front door and onto the circular platform that surrounded the hut. Her stomach still flip-flopped whenever she stepped out here. Yes, she dimly remembered that she had once enjoyed running through the trees. But not *this* high. Up here, when the wind blew, the treetop would actually sway back and forth. A lot. The entire house often slid this way and that, as if in an earthquake. Sometimes at night her hammock would rock, feeling like someone was pushing her. The rest of the family found this quite soothing, like being a baby in a big cradle. But Kirra didn't think she'd ever get used to it. On particularly blustery nights she would hold the fibers of the hammock in a white-knuckle grip until either the wind died down or she passed out from exhaustion, whichever came first.

The first step off the platform was always the hardest. The family had installed helpers, of course. Small loops of rope dangled from surrounding branches to function as reliable hand- and footholds. Planks had been fixed to nearby tree trunks to serve as ladders to branches that were thicker and easier to walk on. But still. That first step took her from the safety of a solidly constructed home to being far above the ground, without any time to get used to the idea.

Kirra inhaled deeply as she oriented herself. The salt caverns were located to the southeast, and Luwan's father had carved the corresponding points of the compass around the rim of the hut's circular roof. Kirra didn't need them at night—still knew how to navigate by the stars—but it certainly helped during the day.

Checking twice to make sure she was headed in the right direction, she leaned forward slowly, grabbed on to two coils of rope for stability, and stepped out. There was always half a moment that took her breath away, when her foot had left the hut's platform and was stretched out over the open air. But that feeling dissipated—mostly, anyway—as soon as her foot was firmly on the branch.

When she had first started living with Luwan's family, she would leave through one of the trapdoors and carefully climb down their home tree all the way to the ground, and then make her way around by walking on the forest floor. But the more she hung out with Luwan, who often went for weeks without ever touching the ground, the more confident she became. And now, even when she was by herself, she saw the value in traveling among the treetops.

Her stomach plunged again when she jumped to the branches of the next tree, her entire body in the air, momentarily unanchored to anything. She always leaped toward the center, the trunk, and kept reminding herself that it wouldn't be the end of the world if she missed a branch for some reason. Luwan had reassured her that it wasn't like stepping off a cliff. She wouldn't plummet straight down two hundred feet to the ground. There were countless branches between her and the forest floor.

"Think of it like this," he had said. "The tree is your friend, and it has a thousand arms that all want to catch you." He had spread out his own arms to demonstrate. "I mean, sure, you might smack into a few of them and fall a bit farther than you wanted to"—here he shrugged—"but, eventually, you'll be able to grab on to one of them and stop yourself from falling. It's, you know, guaranteed."

Kirra had winced. "But wouldn't that hurt?"

"Not as much as hitting the ground—*splat*!" He had punctuated this sentiment by closing his eyes, letting his tongue loll out the side of his mouth, and making death-rattle noises.

Kirra had lunged to give him a little *splat* upside the head for that one, but Luwan had just darted out of her reach and cackled his mischievous little laugh.

But his advice calmed her nerves now as she made her way from branch to branch, tree trunk to tree trunk, heading in the direction of the salt caverns. Kirra was especially thankful that it was still the dry season, although she knew the daily rainstorms would be starting up at any time. A dry branch always felt like a much safer option for supporting and balancing her body weight than a stretch of rain-slick wood.

She had been traveling for less than ten minutes when she heard the muted but unmistakable sounds of a pack of Hook Hunters working its way through the area. Kirra immediately found the thickest surrounding branch and took a seat, leaning back against the tree trunk for comfort. It was unwritten Tree Folk protocol to stay as still as possible when Hook Hunters passed by, as they were able to race through the trees faster than anyone else in the community, and running into someone else up here could have disastrous consequences. But Kirra would have taken a break and peered out from behind the leaves anyway. She loved to watch them whenever she had the chance.

First came the Tracker. She came racing by, two trees over and about twenty feet below, giving Kirra a perfect view.

The speed, as always, was breathtaking. The Tracker held a slender stick in each hand, almost like a small spear except each one ended in a hook instead of a sharpened point. A coiled leather strap was fastened to the straight end, and it looped around the Tracker's wrist to make sure that her hand wouldn't lose its grip.

As the woman dashed along the branches, she constantly worked the hooks above her head in a steady rhythm of activity. They looped over the limbs, providing a split second of traction and steadiness for the Tracker before they were pulled off and transferred to the next spot. She almost looked like a spider, multiple appendages being used in coordination for mobility and stability. It was like a form of running where the arms were just as important as the legs.

Only it isn't really running, Kirra thought. *More like gliding.* For one thing, the Tracker was angling downward and leveraging the pull of gravity, so she was moving faster than Kirra could run at a dead sprint on level ground. And when she needed to reverse course, the Tracker could quickly raise herself several feet in the air by hooking higher and higher branches, pulling herself skyward and running straight up the trunk. She was able to leap from tree to tree with such confidence because the hooks were much more reliable than hands for finding purchase. There were no worries about tender palms being stabbed by a sharp offshoot of branch, and on smooth limbs, the hooks slid right across the surface of the wood, giving the Tracker an exhilarating ride.

Kirra assumed she would only get a brief glimpse of the proceedings, but she was in luck. Whatever creature the Tracker was trailing, it was apparently lingering in the area. The Tracker zoomed past Kirra's perch, but after traversing seven or eight trees in a blur of activity, she slowly started to circle back, creating a loop where Kirra sat on the outer edge.

Tracking prey from this height served the Hook Hunters well. An animal being stalked on the ground could hear a twig snap from a hundred yards away, or catch the tiniest movement out of their peripheral vision, or even smell a hunter if the wind shifted slightly.

But this high up, the animal's keen senses were taken out of play. The Tracker was like a hawk stealthily pursuing its prey from the safety of the sky.

Kirra leaned forward, steadying herself with a strong grip on two neighboring branches, to see if she could identify what was on the Hunters' dinner menu tonight. She watched the Tracker out of the corner of her eye as she scanned what little she could see of the ground far below. The woman with the hooks was narrowing her loop, dropping a few branches lower with each pass, so Kirra trained her vision on the center of that imaginary circle.

There! In a clearing through the leaves, Kirra saw a flash of movement. A boar! A mighty big one, too, from what she could make out at this height.

As soon as the animal popped into view, she heard the Tracker's shrill whistle pierce the forest air. Time for Phase Two.

Kirra watched the surrounding woods, and here came the Spotters—a boy and a girl, not much older than Kirra and so much alike they had to be twins. With their coordinated movements, it seemed as though they'd been born for the job.

The girl popped out of the branches on the eastern side

of the Tracker's tightening circle, while the boy came from the west. They both looked to the Tracker, who was standing on the tip of a branch that was dipping dangerously. She kept one hook around an overhead branch for stability as she leaned out into the open air at an impossible angle. With her other hook, she pointed down at the boar, tracing its movements as it grunted its way through the forest, perhaps trying to hunt down a meal of its own.

The Spotters, taking their cue, started to circle in the air above the animal, nimbly hooking their way from limb to limb, continuing to tighten the loop like a noose. With each pass, they dropped a few branches lower, getting closer and closer to their prey. The Tracker followed suit, staying equidistant between the two Spotters, perfectly triangulating the beast below.

Kirra's heart sped up and she gripped the branches more tightly in anticipation. Almost time for the Main Event. If she was this nervous just watching, she couldn't imagine how her body would be reacting if she were the one about to—

The Kill Signal was given. All three Hunters, much closer together now, pulled a string on the end of each of their hooks, unfurling bright red squares of cloth that flapped in the breeze like flags. They waved them overhead three times and then pointed to the same spot on the ground. From her bird's-eye vantage point above them, the space between their bodies looked like a tunnel leading right to their prey below.

Kirra looked up, and here came the final member of the team. The Pouncer.

If it had looked like the Tracker was gliding, then the Pouncer was flying. He dropped out of the sky like a stone, falling impossible lengths through the open air before hooking a branch or two in order to shift direction or control his speed.

He zoomed past Kirra in a dizzying rush, but completely silent, just like a diving bird of prey.

She watched as he plunged, steering himself in between his team members, and dropped right through their triangle of flags. As he became a tiny doll figure far below, he hooked the lowest level of branches, then let himself fall the rest of the way to the ground. Kirra could just faintly make out the terrified squeal of the boar, which must never have known it was being stalked.

The Tracker and two Spotters tied up their flags and then dropped to the ground themselves, ready to help with the butchering, or to make a travois if they had to drag their prize any distance. Whichever was the case, their families would be eating very well tonight.

Kirra stood and stretched, working the kinks out of her legs. She really shouldn't have taken the time to watch all of that—dinner was going to be even later—but she just couldn't resist the show.

She started to make her way southeasterly again, only

now, after watching the fluidly coordinated movements of the Hook Hunters, she felt like a clumsy toddler inching her way along.

And the thought of all that boar meat was making her hungry. The soup in the pot back home would be good, she was certain, but it was no substitute for a fresh haunch of wild pig, slow-roasted over an open flame. She could almost smell it.

Kirra was so caught up in her dinner fantasies, she didn't take careful note of her surroundings. She stepped on a branch that was rigged to work as a trip wire. A great stone dropped from a hidden perch in the tree, pulling a rope that made the net cinch up into a ball. With her inside.

She'd been captured.

11

KIRRA WAS DANGLING UPSIDE DOWN, her body pressed against the tightly woven net, twigs and leaves mashing into her face. One arm was pinned to her side, but she was able to work her free hand up to clear a space so she could peek through a hole.

A man ascended the trunk, moving with the liquid grace of a jungle cat. His clothing was all dull greens and dirty browns, allowing him to blend in seamlessly with leaf and limb. He was peering up at her through a screen of tightly braided hair, and his scarred hands and feet instinctively found grips for climbing while his eyes never left the net.

When the man reached Kirra's branch, he nimbly hoisted himself up and withdrew a long, sharp cutting stone from the waistband of his shorts. Kirra was helpless to do anything but watch as he got closer and closer.

"Hey, Mome."

The man bent over and squinted into the net.

"Oh. Hello, Kirra." He gave her a little wave. "I was hoping to find the leopard that has been patrolling these parts."

"So sorry to disappoint you."

"Oh well. He'll be back." Mome shrugged and sat down cross-legged on the wide branch. "And what are you doing on this fine afternoon?"

Kirra shook her head. Or rather, she tried to. Being trussed up like this did not lend itself to much mobility. She settled for an eye roll. "Well, at the moment I seem to be stuck in this tree."

"My, my. So you do." Mome's brow crinkled, matching the deep wrinkles that lined the rest of his face. He gestured at Kirra's predicament like he had just noticed she was incapacitated. "And why are you like this?"

"You know why."

Mome raised one eyebrow in a question.

"*You* did this," Kirra said. "This is your net. You caught me. In a trap. Like a wild animal."

"Well . . . perhaps you should not have wandered so close

to my home." Mome shrugged. "Like a wild animal."

"That's hardly fair, Mome. You change the location of your home every month or so. It's hard to keep up."

He waggled a finger at her. "One can never be too careful. I've seen many things in this life, young lady." Mome bent down and reached through the holes in the net to clear away some leaves, revealing more of Kirra's face. He studied her for several moments. "Do you know what I think?"

Kirra tried to blow a stray lock of hair out of her face. "What?"

"I think you have sad eyes. They've always told me that you've seen some things in this life, as well." After a long silence he added, "Yes?"

Kirra looked away. "You know I don't talk about things like that. The past."

"But we cannot know the future. So what else is there to talk about except the past?"

"How about we talk about you getting me out of this net in the very near future?"

"Oh, my. So feisty." He leaned forward and squinted at her, then poked tentatively at an elbow that was sticking out of the net. "Are you sure you're not a leopard?"

Kirra just rolled her eyes again. Mome chuckled and reached up with his cutting tool, hacked through a section of rope, and the entire net came apart. Kirra was unceremoniously deposited onto the broad branch with a thump.

"Oof." She clambered to her feet, rubbing her lower back where she had smacked the limb.

"Hmm. Strange. I thought leopards always landed on their paws."

"I'm not your leopard, Mome."

He tilted his head this way and that, chin in his hand, studying her. Finally he gave her a dismissive wave. "Oh, I suppose not. But you should come to my humble house anyway and share a drink with me. I'm working on a new concoction with honey and berries. You will love it!" Mome talked with his hands and his eyes went all crinkly when he was excited.

Kirra was still dusting herself off. "I would do that, Mome, really. But I need to get to the salt caverns before dinner. And I'm late already."

She turned to step away, but Mome took her gently by the shoulders. "We have not chatted in a long time, and I have plenty of salt at the moment. How about this: You take as much as you need, and then spend the time you saved visiting with old Mome."

Kirra chewed on her lip, weighing the offer. It would be nice not to have to haul herself all the way to the caverns. And Mome always treated her with kindness. But still . . . talking to him was like walking through a maze where a Memory Trap lurked behind every corner, because he was also—

"It's called borrowing from a neighbor, Kirra, and in

some parts of this wide world, it's actually quite a common practice."

She looked down. "I know about borrowing," she mumbled. "And I know about neighbors."

Mome gave her a gentle smile. "I had a feeling you did." The old man leaned in and tapped her forehead. "I think that a time when you learned to borrow from neighbors is part of your story."

Kirra turned her head away.

"Come now." He nudged her in the ribs. "If you and I start acting neighborly and borrowing from each other, who knows? The practice might catch on with these folks." Mome gestured at the surrounding forest.

Kirra turned to face him again; that was another reason she had always liked this man, ever since she first arrived. He spoke to her as a fellow outsider. Like her, Mome hadn't been born into the Tree Folk, so the two of them shared an unlikely bond.

"Hmm . . . how far away is your new house?"

Mome pointed directly overhead. "We're practically there. This"—he kicked at the fallen net—"is my last line of defense against all things leopardy."

He reached up and disappeared into the leaves above. Kirra sighed and followed. She saw his "house" immediately, though it was a pretty bare-bones operation: thatched roof woven among the branches to keep the rainfall away, a single hammock, and a few shelves harboring Mome's meager accumulation of possessions.

Soon Kirra was sitting in the guest chair: a bunch of thick, soft moss that had been stuffed into the V created by two branches emerging from the trunk at the same spot. She was able to lie back and relax a bit, holding a wooden cup of the honey juice that Mome had whipped up. It was delicious.

"Okay, this is pretty cozy," she admitted. "But why do you change houses so often, Mome?"

Sipping from his own cup, the older man tilted his head and gave her question some thought for a few moments. He always did that. Most adults answered right away, even if they weren't completely sure about what they were saying. It was like they just wanted to get the conversation over with as quickly as possible. Mome taking time to weigh her words was proof that he took them seriously.

"Well . . . I suppose it's because if you work really hard to build a perfect house, and you spend all your time filling it with this and that . . . it becomes easy to confuse what truly belongs there with what doesn't."

"What do you mean?"

He turned back, fixing her with his soft gaze. "It's the people in a house that matter, not the house or the possessions. Never the *things*."

Kirra nodded. Sometimes when he said something, it hit

her in the core of her being and sounded right without her having to think about it.

Mome glanced away, looking absently at the surrounding trees. His face fell a bit as he stared at nothing in particular, as if dismayed by a distant memory. When he spoke again, his voice was much quieter. "And also because you can never be sure when you might have to leave your home quickly. Not being too attached makes that easier to do."

Kirra flinched as if he had reared back to strike her.

The older man noticed the reaction. He gently placed a hand on her arm. "Sometimes when I say things to you, I can see storm clouds roll across your eyes." He patted her for a while, letting Kirra gather herself. Finally, Mome said, "Will you at last tell me what happened to you? Share part of your story with me—where you came from, perhaps? I may be able to help you, Kirra."

She just shook her head. "There's nothing to tell."

"Everyone has a story."

"I don't like stories," she said quickly.

"Oh, I'm so sorry to hear that." Mome sighed deeply. "They are what make us different from the animals, you know?"

"What are you talking about?" Kirra knew she had to step carefully. Mome could surround her with Memory Traps before she even knew what was happening. This could end very, very badly.

But still . . . it had been so long since she'd heard a new story. Or even heard anyone say something good about stories. Salt was not the only thing that the Tree Folk failed to share with one another.

Mome leaned forward from his perch in the hammock and gestured to the forest floor far below. "I'm sure you've noticed that the animals are much better suited for life in this hard world than we are. Warm fur coats, sharp teeth, claws that work like a handful of tools, the power to run much faster, or jump higher, or even fly. They should be in charge of everything!"

Kirra might be nervous about where this conversation was headed, but it was always a treat to watch Mome get worked up about something. His eyes shone like they were sparkling in the light of a campfire, and his fingers danced in the air as he gestured to emphasize his points.

"But the beasts do not have stories, and that is our one advantage." He grinned and waggled his eyebrows at her. "Stories pass on hard-earned knowledge to the next generation, they gather communities together for the telling, and they show us what life is like in other tribes in distant lands, even make us *feel* what those people might be feeling. It's like magic for your mind!" Mome clapped as if his body needed an outlet for all of this joy.

Kirra couldn't help but smile a little at his enthusiasm,

but she kept it hidden by training her face downward, pretending to study the ground below.

Mome leaned even closer, trying to establish eye contact with her. "And perhaps most importantly, they can teach us about ourselves."

Kirra allowed her mind to flash backward, only for a moment. She saw a man, a woman, and a small boy sitting beside her around a campfire. The man—faceless, like the others—was telling a silly story and the rest of them were cracking up, throwing their heads back with laughter and clutching one another. The woman turned in her direction and—

No. Kirra shut that memory down hard.

Finally, she shrugged and looked back at Mome. Her voice was very quiet. "And sometimes stories are just for fun."

"Exactly!" Mome broke into a giggle that made him sound like a much younger man. "That is indeed the truth, and isn't it wonderful? The leopard may have the speed and the strength and the teeth and the claws, but when does he ever have a little fun?" Mome shook his head, still letting loose unself-consciously with his childlike snickering. "Do you know any just-for-fun stories, meerkat?"

She slurped the last of her drink and handed the empty cup to Mome. "I think I should be getting back home now."

Mome grabbed the cup, and before Kirra could haul

herself out of the comfy seat, he refilled it. "Okay, the past is out. Stories are out. I understand." He wafted the drink under her nose. It smelled so good, she found herself accepting it. "Let us talk about the present, then," Mome went on. "How are you getting along with your Tree Family these days?"

Kirra leaned back and sighed. This was also difficult to speak about, but it was definitely preferable to trying to describe anything that might have taken place Before.

"Things are . . . Oh, they're the same, I suppose." She shook her head. "Luwan is as crazy as ever."

Mome grinned. "I'm glad you two have each other. I have not seen him buzzing around here recently, so please tell him I said hello."

"Catch him in one of your leopard traps and tell him yourself. He's the one who deserves that kind of treatment, not me."

"I might just do that." Mome took a deep breath, and his grin faltered a bit. "And Luwan's parents? Any developments there?"

Kirra shrugged. "Not really. Loba concentrates on the hunt while Maham does the fishing and foraging. They are a good team. I see them at mealtimes and in the evenings, especially if it's cold and the family is sitting around the fire."

Mome nodded. "And they are kind to you?"

"Always," Kirra said quickly. "They have provided everything I need, ever since the first day I got here. Never a harsh word. Not once. I owe them everything."

"I know, I know." Mome held up his palms in a placating gesture. "They take very good care of your physical needs. I'm just wondering, young Kirra"—Mome tapped his chest—"are they able to take care of your heart, as well?"

She gave him a look. "I don't need that, Mome. Just because I don't talk about where I came—"

"Everyone needs heart care, meerkat. It's a simple fact, and nothing to be ashamed of."

She stared at him. She had not cried since she'd arrived in this forest, and she did not intend to start now.

"I know that. And they try. Really. It's just that . . . we've never made a real connection . . . because, well . . ."

"You come from somewhere else," Mome said softly.

It took her several moments to answer. "Yes."

"And that makes them uneasy."

Kirra swallowed heavily. "Yes." She chewed on her lip in thought. "But doesn't . . . I mean, doesn't everyone around here come from somewhere else? Originally?"

"Why do you ask?"

"The families . . . they look different from each other. And they sound different, too."

"Indeed. The first Tree Folk did come from many places. It's a patchwork community of sorts." Mome sighed and poured them each a bit more of the berry drink. "You have more in common with these people than you think."

Kirra was silent but made a *keep going* gesture by twirling her fingers in a circle.

"As you know, communities can come to an end for many reasons. Resources dry up, or a flood displaces a tribe, or sometimes, war breaks out—" Mome saw Kirra wince at that, and so he hurried along. "Whatever the reason, sometimes survivors need to find a new place. That's what brought all these different people to the forest."

Mome gestured to his little hideaway. "Since they were running from something unpleasant, they decided to hide up here in the branches. Create a safe haven for themselves. Or at least make it so they feel safe."

Mome let that soak in for a while. Eventually Kirra looked back up at him. "So that's why this community . . . isn't like one big family? Why people are polite but not, you know, friendly?"

"That's exactly right. They might share when they need to—in an emergency—but they don't share what's truly important. They don't share themselves. They're too afraid."

His words, though spoken gently, crashed against Kirra's ears. He might have been explaining how this community works, but he could have just as easily been describing how she had felt for the last four years.

Mome paused and tapped her on the forehead again. "Like

you, they're not only afraid of others . . . They're also afraid of themselves. They are trying to forget their own stories. And since they've been here longer than you—a few generations, perhaps, long enough to see you as an outsider—many of them have succeeded." He sat back again. "But a community without stories is a sad place," he went on. "It has no past, and so it has no future."

Kirra didn't answer. Sometimes not crying took all her concentration.

Mome looked at her silently with sad but kind eyes. He didn't say *Everything will be okay* like most adults did when kids felt terrible. He allowed her to feel what she was feeling, and Kirra was reminded again of why she liked being around him so much.

Finally, the older man spoke. "If you're not careful, meerkat, you, too, may forget where you came from. You may forget your story entirely, as these people have."

She sighed heavily. "That's the plan."

Mome shook his head. But then he stood and stretched, and lifted Kirra's pouch from the branch where she had hung it. He found his salt bowl on a rough plank that served as a shelf, dumped the contents inside the pouch, and handed it to Kirra.

"Come with me. Before you return home, I would like to show you something."

12

ENCOUNTERING TREE FOLK while traveling through the woods was eerie. Kirra didn't think she would ever get used to it.

Everyone dressed in forest-friendly earth tones, like Mome, so they blended right in with their surroundings. And while she used to fancy herself as someone who could quietly make her way through the trees, Kirra had quickly learned she was no match for those who'd been born two hundred feet off the ground in a windstorm. These people had grown up being part of the very fabric of the forest, just as much as the birds or the beasts or the rain that dripped from the leaves during the wet season.

But mostly it was the way the Tree Folk acted, she supposed. The way they kept to themselves. Outside the Tree Folk community, when you passed a person on a trail or the road, they acknowledged you somehow. A smile, a wave, or perhaps just a quick nod. Something that conveyed the message *Hey there, we're both people who happen to be out walking near each other today!*

But the Tree Folk rarely recognized your presence at all unless you looked at them directly. Several times Kirra had been working her way across a delicate branch, searching for handholds and testing the limb to see if it would carry her weight, blithely assuming she was the only one in this stretch of the forest . . . and then she would turn to see someone perched, silent and nearly invisible, right next to her on a neighboring branch. It gave her the willies every time. The person was never being weird or menacing or anything— just politely waiting for her to pass so he didn't interfere with her navigation of the tree—but it was still unnerving.

It was a bit better traversing the forest with Mome, as he was always better at spotting—or perhaps sensing—these fellow travelers, so at least he provided Kirra some warning.

She was walking on a thick branch behind him when he said, "Is this still the best way to get to the clearing by the

The bonfire exploded, the flames leaping twenty, thirty, forty feet in the air.

As Kirra emerged from the tunnel onto a ledge inside the volcano crater, she had to admit it was good to be back home.

Cobar would never have guessed that any of these natives were
clever enough, but they had made a nest within the crater walls. . . .

Kirra could see the swollen river rising to meet her.

"There is something I want to show you," Mome said.

The sight of Luwan there, trussed up like a wild animal and completely helpless, made Kirra want to charge in.

This was what Kirra had been born to do.

The two groups met in an explosion of violence.

lake? The one with the rocky ridge at one end where a fisher might sit comfortably and throw out a line?"

Kirra scrunched up her eyebrows. *Why would he be asking me?* she wondered. She opened her mouth to say she had no idea, then realized that Mome was actually talking to three men who were silently passing them among the branches.

The oldest one, his beard flecked with gray, pointed into the distance. "A fire last week made travel treacherous to the south. Better to loop around this way. The distance may be greater, but you will save time."

"I appreciate that. Thank you."

"Yes. Good travels."

And then all three men slipped away into the heart of the forest without a sound. Kirra thought about how this was typical of all interactions with Tree Folk who were not part of one's immediate inner circle. There was no animosity at all, no fear that these people might rob you or attack you or otherwise take any advantage from the encounter. But there was no warmth, either, no sense that it mattered to them whether you reached your destination, and certainly no inclination that they might want to join you and chat along the way. The meeting happened by chance, information was exchanged, and then the meeting ended.

But maybe that was starting to change a bit with the younger members of the Tree Folk. After all, Luwan had his little group of friends that he ran around with. And while the more established Hook Hunter groups were made up of only family members, she knew that some of the newer ones held open trials once a year and would take new recruits from anywhere in the community, as long as they had the skill and the nerve.

"Something on your mind?" Mome said, pulling her out of her thoughts about the future of Tree Folk society.

Kirra shook her head. "So . . . are you taking me on a fishing trip?" she asked.

"What? Oh, no. I just need to find that clearing with the lake. There is something I want to show you. We're almost there."

Mome started to descend straight down the tree. Kirra followed and felt the familiar twinges of relief as they got closer to the forest floor. She simply felt safer on the ground.

The clearing was beautiful, and she did remember being here before, with Luwan, daring each other to dive from atop the ridge. Her arrival in the Tree Folk community was mostly lost to her recollection in a hazy mix of confusion and fear and things that she didn't want to think or talk about at the time. But coming here was one of her first good memories of this place.

The clearing allowed in much more sunlight than the dense forest, so it was one of the brightest spots Kirra had seen in this area. And the surrounding trees gave the lake a beautiful emerald tint. The water was warm and felt like silk on bare skin, and if you floated on your back and stayed very still, the fish would start jumping all around you. It had felt like a welcome to her new home when that happened. If the people weren't overly enthusiastic about her arrival, at least the fish had accepted her as part of the landscape.

This little oasis was also one of the few places where you saw Tree Folk from different families out in the open at the same time. But still, they were separate. Small groups of three or four huddled around the perimeter of the lake, throwing out fishing lines, or wading in the water to cool off, or filling buckets with water to take back home.

There were about two dozen Tree Folk out here now, scattered around the great open space. Kirra watched them, the evening sun fading but still warm on her face, until Mome took her gently by the hand and led her to a jumbled pile of rocks at one end of the clearing. She couldn't imagine what was out here that he might need to show her.

Kirra gave the older man a look. "I'm not the bait for your next leopard trap, am I?"

Mome chuckled. "No, meerkat. I want to introduce you to something else."

As they neared the rocks, Mome slowed. Then he dropped to one knee and Kirra did the same. He pointed ahead and whispered to her, "Do you see that? Underneath that ledge of stone there?"

Kirra craned her neck forward and squinted. There was a dark mound a few feet high. "Is it a nest or pod of some kind?"

Mome nodded. "It is. And do you see anything unusual about it?"

Kirra tilted her head this way and that, studying the little knoll. "Not particularly. Looks like a small animal lives in there, or a family of them, maybe? But nothing seems out of the ordinary."

Mome waved her forward. "Let's get a bit closer."

As she got nearer, Kirra saw that the surface of the structure was . . . moving? *Writhing.* How was that possible? What kind of a material would do that with no discernible breeze? She took a few steps closer and saw—

"Wait—are those ants?"

Mome smiled. "They are."

Kirra got even closer and dropped down to one knee again for a better view. "That entire nest is made up of nothing but ants?" It looked like there were a million of them swarming around to make this structure. Their legs and bodies were linked together so tightly it was no wonder it had taken her so long to notice them.

She pointed at the middle of the mass. "What's inside?"

"The queen. And all of her eggs. These are the colony's most prized possessions, and every member does their part to protect them."

"How long do they stay like that?"

Mome shrugged. "As long as they need to. In the morning, many will break away from the nest and go off in raiding parties to find food to bring back. When this area becomes unsuitable, the whole crew will move to a different part of the forest. They can reassemble into this protective covering for the queen at a moment's notice. The structure is called a bivouac, so I call these the bivouac ants. Every ant knows its job and does it well, and their colony prospers."

Kirra whistled in appreciation. "That's amazing."

Mome picked up a fallen branch. "Watch this." He leaned forward and gently poked the stick into the middle of the heap of ants. Kirra was afraid he was going to squish hundreds of them, but the ants instantaneously rearranged themselves to allow the stick to dip right inside the structure, like it was sinking into a thick liquid.

When the stick was sunk in about a foot or so, Mome started to stir it around slowly. She was worried he would ruin the structure, scattering the ants everywhere, but the little insects shifted and moved together, as if controlled by one mind, and the stick was able to travel unimpeded through the mound. When Mome let go, the stick stood straight up, the ants having absorbed the foreign object into their space.

"Whoa," Kirra breathed.

Mome nodded. "They are remarkable creatures." He gripped the stick again and pulled it out. It was clean, not a single ant clinging to its surface, and the hole it had created disappeared as the ants swarmed to fill the empty area. Soon it was a solid structure once again.

Kirra shook her head in wonder. She reached out hesitantly, as if to touch the mound, but pulled her hand back. "It's beautiful in a way, isn't it? I mean, I never thought I would say that about a million bugs, but it is."

Mome gave her a long look with his kind eyes. "I think it's quite telling that you find beauty in this, young Kirra."

"Really? Why?"

"You and I are similar," he said. "We're both outsiders."

"Yes . . ." She didn't need the reminder.

"I figure," Mome went on, "that after ten years here I've gotten as close to the Tree Folk as anyone from the outside is going to get."

He gestured around the clearing, at the individual small groups of people clustered together. "These people mean one another absolutely no harm . . . but neither are they in a rush to do for one another."

Kirra nodded. He was putting his finger on something that she could never talk to the family about. "Yes. That's it exactly." She chewed on her lip, deep in thought, not entirely sure how to phrase the next part. "And it's, well, it's *unusual*, isn't it? I mean, you think that, too, right? It's not just me."

"You and I find it unusual, but that's only because we were raised differently."

She pieced it together. "So they don't notice this might seem unusual. Because it's what they've always known."

"That's right."

"But . . ." Kirra searched for the right words. "Isn't it . . . I mean, no matter how you were raised . . . isn't it just *easier* to share? A more natural way for people to behave?"

"When you're used to it, yes, of course," Mome said. "But if it's not what you're accustomed to, sharing is scary."

"Scary? How?"

Again, Mome took the time to give her question real thought. "Because people are worried they aren't going to get the amount they think they deserve."

"Right, but it never works out totally equal like that. Sometimes you get a little more, so next time you take a little less. It's just common sense."

When Mome smiled it was with his whole face, not just his mouth. "The fact that you know all this so well, young Kirra, that it is such a part of you, makes me think you used to live in a place that worked like this." He gestured at the bivouac structure.

Kirra snapped her head to look directly at him, a flash of resentment in her eyes. "Is that why you brought me here? To trick me into talking about it?"

Mome shook his head gently. "No, meerkat. I only wanted to—"

"Can't people just live their lives in peace?" She stood up, brushed herself off. "Maybe I prefer being someplace where people don't have to share everything."

Mome stood and tenderly placed his hands on her shoulders. "I have lived for many years, Kirra. I have traveled far and wide and experienced a great many things. I know that some communities . . . well, they come to an end, like a tree dying in the forest. And also like a tree, they can cause a lot of damage when they fall."

Suddenly, Kirra felt very tired.

"That's the problem with not sharing your stories, with shutting them out." Mome gently brushed tears from her cheeks. "It can be comforting to block bad memories. So comforting that it feels like the right thing to do . . ."

Kirra nodded slowly.

"But when we do that," Mome continued, "we also shut out all the good. And those are the things that help us heal."

Kirra's heart was racing, even though she was standing perfectly still. It felt like a torrent of memories was threatening to drown her, and Mome wanted to open the dam.

But she would not let him. She pushed his hands away.

"You don't know anything about me," she said.

Kirra turned and fled into the forest.

13

WHEN SHE ARRIVED BACK HOME, panting for breath after climbing two hundred feet, Loba and Maham were already there. They had gotten the fire going again, and the house smelled like fresh stew. Her stomach rumbled.

"Hello there," said Maham, stirring the bubbling pot. She offered Kirra a smile. "I'm glad to see you home safe."

"Thank you. I'm sorry to be late." Kirra took the pouch off her back.

"Where have you been?" asked Loba. He was hanging his hunting cloak—mottled with greens and browns to blend in with the forest—on a hook near the fire. It was damp, so perhaps he'd been stalking prey in one of the swamps. Kirra allowed herself to hope that maybe there'd be a night of crocodile steaks this week. That had become one of her favorite meals since coming to this place.

"I had to go get salt. We were running low."

"Oh, that's good. I didn't want to say anything"—Maham smiled at her as she held up the ladle—"but this dish could definitely use it."

"Did you have any trouble getting to the caverns?" Loba asked. "I haven't been over that way since the fire."

"Oh . . . I ended up not having to go out there. I saw Mome, and he said we could have some of his."

Loba stroked his beard as he studied her. Most adult men in the Tree Folk community grew them long. Kirra had always thought they looked like the stringy moss that hung off trees by the swamp. *Maybe he should dye his beard green to enhance his camouflage*, she thought.

Normally she would have said that out loud, but the look on Loba's face made it clear he was not in a joking mood.

"Why did you go to his house and not the caverns?"

Kirra shrugged, trying to make it seem casual. "I just ran into him and told him where I was headed, and he offered to let us use his supply." She purposely left out the part about being caught up in the leopard trap. Loba did not need another reason to wonder about Mome.

Besides, Loba had a way of making Kirra feel guilty, even when she hadn't done anything wrong. Were all fathers like that . . . or just adoptive ones who maybe weren't that crazy about the fact they ever met you in the first place?

"How much did he give you?"

Kirra held up her pouch by the strings and gently shook it so he could guess how much was inside. Then she handed the pouch to Maham, who was clearly grateful to have something to do during this conversation. She immediately opened it and started seasoning the stew. Loba remained quiet.

Kirra looked back and forth between them. "Did I do something I wasn't supposed to?"

Loba sighed heavily. He raked fingers through his damp hair to dry it out. Then he pulled his long locks back and tied them with a leather strap.

"Look, I'm not saying you necessarily did anything *wrong*, Kirra. It's just that we don't truly know Mome. He's not part of this family. What will he want in return?"

"Nothing."

Loba gave her a look.

"Nothing, really! I mean, the next time I'm at the salt caverns, I'll fill an extra pouch and bring it to his house to repay him for the kindness. But he wasn't trying to get anything else."

Loba stroked his beard some more. "Did he try to fill

your head with more of his stories? He's not from here, you know."

Kirra looked at the wooden floor with eyes that had threatened to burn with tears again. "I'm not from here, either," she said quietly.

"Oh, honey," said Maham, "that's not what he meant. Loba was merely trying—"

"He's not like you, Kirra. When Mome came here, he didn't join a family, didn't learn our ways, didn't try to blend in. He's always just kept to himself on the fringe."

Isn't that what we're all doing? Kirra didn't dare say. *Isn't this entire community one big fringe?*

Loba straightened up, cleared his throat. "I'll need to think about this. I don't know how much I want you talking to him anymore."

Fine. Kirra could relate. After their conversation by the lake, she wasn't sure how much more she wanted to keep talking to Mome, either.

Maham tried to break the awkward silence. "Well, I'm sorry you couldn't go straight to the caverns. I hope the rainy season gets here soon. It's long overdue, but when it comes, we won't have to worry about any more wildfires."

"The rainy season might not be here yet, but *I* am!" a voice said.

All three of them jumped in surprise, Maham dropping the ladle and splashing soup on herself.

They looked up to see Luwan's head poking down through the hole in the roof, dodging this way and that to avoid the smoke rising through it. Kirra felt relief wash through her. Luwan's antics could be annoying at times, but he had a knack for defusing tense family situations, and she was glad he had shifted attention away from that uncomfortable exchange.

"By the gods, son, can't you come through the front door like a normal person?" Kirra couldn't help noticing that even when Loba spoke gruffly to Luwan, there was still more tenderness in his tone than when he was telling her something nice.

Luwan's face disappeared. "Normal is boring!" he called, and then they could hear him thumping down the roof until he appeared in the open doorway. He knocked primly on the edge of the door and spread his arms wide. "Is this normal enough?" He flashed Kirra a grin.

Loba shook his head. "Just get in here and wash up. It's time for dinner."

Maham folded the table down from the wall, and they all gathered around it after filling their wooden bowls.

"Mmm. This is good soup, Kirra," Maham said. "Thank you for making it for everyone."

Loba, mouth full, grunted his approval.

Kirra smiled. "Thank you. And many thanks for trapping the meat so I could make it."

Loba nodded at her.

The rest of the meal was eaten largely in silence. This was normal for most of the family, but not Luwan. He usually talked so much that Kirra was amazed he could actually finish his dinner at the same time, especially since he seemed to eat twice as much as anyone else.

She knew what his silence likely meant, though—there was something he wanted from his parents, and he was waiting for the right time to ask. She would have bet any of her possessions on it. The thought made her stomach a little queasy, though; just as Luwan could defuse any volatile situation, he could also ignite one in record time.

Luwan picked up his bowl, slurped the last bit of soup, smacked his lips appreciatively, and set the dish back on the table with a *clack*. Then he stretched his arms over his head, let out a satisfied "Ahh!" and looked around the table. "So, parents, there's something I want to talk to you about."

Maham glanced out of the corner of her eye at Loba, who merely sighed and pushed himself back in his seat. He crossed his arms over his chest and regarded his son with a stoic expression. Kirra wasn't the only one who knew how to read Luwan.

"So I've been thinking—"

Loba grunted at that.

"We should really be taking more advantage of this unusually long dry season."

Loba and Maham shared a look. "And . . . how do you think we should be doing that?" his mother asked.

"Well, after the rains come, you know how wild the river will get. All that turbulent whitewater, and so deep? Dangerous, some may say."

Maham cleared her throat. "Yes, we know this, Luwan. It's why the river marks the natural border of our lands, a buffer between us and the tribes that lie beyond."

Loba pointed at his son. "It's also the reason you're not allowed to go down there. We give you free rein of the forest and any lands that lie to the east, but you are to stay away from there."

Kirra shifted uncomfortably in her seat. She didn't like this talk about the river. It was one long, winding, overflowing Memory Trap. Everyone at the table knew what had happened the last time Luwan snuck down there without permission.

Luwan held up both hands in a placating gesture. "I know, I know. And I completely agree with you. But . . . have you seen it lately? It's so low, I bet I could wade right across it to the other side."

"Not a chance." Loba slowly shook his head. "We've talked about this already. The riverbed could be unstable—like quicksand that could suck you right under. There could be holes you can't see beneath the surface. Or currents that could sweep you away. No. Not going to happen. It wouldn't matter even if it had been ten years since the last rain."

"Oh, of course, Father. *Of course* I would never try to walk across." Luwan's exaggerated tone made it clear doing that was the furthest thing from his mind.

"Well then . . ." Maham set her spoon down and pushed the empty bowl away. "Why are we talking about this?"

"Okay. Please listen before you decide anything. You promise?"

Loba's expression said it all: Parents did not make blanket promises to their children, especially regarding unknown requests.

Luwan forged ahead. "Right. So you know how my friend Teeha is really good at building things? She's amazing." He looked at his parents, an expectant expression on his face, as if seeking confirmation for this fact.

Loba just twirled his finger in the *keep going* gesture.

"Well, she hasn't been hanging out with us much the last month, because she's been working on some secret project. But she finally showed it to us today, and it's unbelievable. It's this enormous raft—big enough to hold all of our friends. It's really sturdy, and we were thinking that—"

Loba pushed himself back from the table and stood up, giving his son a dismissive wave. All he said was a simple no.

"But, Father, I need—"

"The discussion is closed."

"But I'd be doing it for the family!" Luwan jumped to his

feet to plead his case. "Think of the fishing spots we could find, places no one has ever been. I could bring home enough to provide dinners for a month. Or more!" He looked to his mother for support, but her head was bowed as she collected the bowls from the table and stacked them up.

Loba retrieved his cloak from the hook, patted it to make sure it was dry, then slipped it on. "I need to fix a few loose planks on one of the trees to the northwest." He picked up a lantern and moved toward the door.

"Father, are you even listening? We wouldn't go far, I promise. I would be back in just two days. Three at the most."

Loba stopped in the doorway and turned around. "Listen to me well, Luwan. We do not go into the river. The forest is vast. It is enough."

"But think of all the fish I could—"

"Have you ever known a hungry night in your life?" Loba's voice was very calm now. Quiet and even. Kirra found it much more unnerving than when he raised his voice.

Luwan threw his hands in the air in exasperation. "What?"

"Have you ever, even one time, gone to sleep hungry?"

Luwan stared back at his father. Finally he said, "No."

"Exactly. We have everything we need right here." He turned to walk through the doorway. "You will stay away from the river," he said over his shoulder as he walked out of the hut.

The silence was heavy after Loba left. Maham busied herself with cleaning the bowls and the cooking pot. Kirra patched some clothes that had gotten ripped while she was climbing, and Luwan sat quietly with his back up against the wall. He went to his hammock early without saying good night to anyone.

But later, when Kirra climbed down through a trapdoor to get into her sleep sling, she found Luwan awake in his with hands behind his head, whistling a jaunty little tune. Kirra hung a lantern on the hook between their two hammocks. The two had slept near each other ever since she had arrived.

"Seems like you're in a good mood," she whispered. "Especially considering, you know . . ." Kirra made a face and gestured to the hut above them to indicate the tense conversation after dinner.

Luwan stopped whistling and raised one eyebrow at her. "Don't tell me you actually believed all that?" he whispered.

"What? Of course. But you . . . Wait, what do you mean?"

"Father would never let me go out on a raft on that river. Not in a million moons."

"I know! So why did you ask?"

Luwan *tsk-tsk*ed and slowly shook his head in mock sadness. "Oh, Kirra. So much to learn about negotiating."

"What do you mean?"

"Come on, it's a setup. All part of the game that kids and

their parents play." He shifted in his hammock so he was lying on his side, facing her. "Step one: I ask them for something impossible. Step two: They say no. Step three: I put up a bit of a fight and pretend that it crushes me."

Kirra raised one eyebrow. "So far, doesn't seem like the best plan."

Luwan smirked. "But all that leads to step four, when I ask them for what I *really* want, and since they feel so bad about saying no today, it increases the chances they say yes tomorrow."

"Oh. So what is it you really want?"

"I'll show you tomorrow. Promise."

Kirra was curious, but she knew better than to ask him any more about it. Luwan loved his little surprises, and she would just have to find out when he was ready to tell her.

They lay there quietly for a while, listening to the night noises of the forest. A breeze rustled the leaves in a pleasant way; it wasn't strong enough to sway the hammocks.

Finally, she said, "Did Teeha really build a raft?"

"Yes, and it's amazing. I swear, that girl could build anything."

She felt a pang of jealousy. She was glad Luwan had friends—she didn't expect him to hang around with her at home all day—but sometimes she wished she could do something to make her seem like more than just the poor victim he rescued. "Why didn't you tell me about it?"

He shrugged. "I didn't want to worry you. And besides . . . you don't really like to talk about the river, you know? You never go down there."

"You heard your father. We're not supposed to."

"I know, but all the kids do, sometimes. Except you. In fact, I don't think you have been down there at all since—"

"I *know* the last time I was at the river, Luwan."

"Right. Sorry."

Silence stretched out between them for a bit until Luwan cleared his throat. "Okay. Time to get some sleep. Tomorrow's going to be an exciting day." He flopped over on his side.

Exciting how? Kirra wondered, but Luwan was already softly snoring. She marveled—with more than a little envy—at how untroubled a mind he must have to be able to turn it off that easily.

14

KIRRA WOKE TO THE SOUND OF BIRDSONG, the soft morning light revealing the forest home around her. Slowly coming back to consciousness in the fresh open air was one of her favorite parts of living here.

Luwan's hammock hung empty beside her. That was unusual—he liked to sleep late. But as Kirra slowly reached above her head with both hands, working the sleep-sore kinks out of her back, she remembered that he was planning to ask his parents for something today. So he was probably currying favor with them right now by getting an early start on his studies.

The Tree Folk had no community school—no community services of any kind, for that matter—so each family was in charge of teaching its own kids. Maham took this very seriously, drilling them on things like horticulture, the medicinal uses of plants, and food preservation every morning. The afternoons were spent farther afield, hunting and trapping and building and exploring.

But when Kirra finally pulled herself out of the sleep sling and climbed up through the trapdoor, Luwan was all by himself in the hut, slurping leftover stew for breakfast.

"You're finally up! Good. I was just about to wake you. We have things to do."

"We do? Where are Loba and Maham?"

"They both went to the swamp. Father needed Mother's help today. Have you ever tried to carry a crocodile? Those things are heavy."

"So no studies this morning? Really?"

Luwan shrugged and tried to pull off an innocent expression. "Well . . . if someone had left a note with parental instructions on it next to a window . . . I mean, who's to say that a breeze didn't come by and, *whoosh*, snatch that note right off the sill and send it sailing away into the forest, never to be seen again? Things like that happen all the time. The world is a cruel and windy place."

Kirra rolled her eyes. "You're going to get us in trouble."

Luwan waved away her concerns. "Nah. They'll be so tired when they get back that they will have forgotten all about it." He grabbed a long, thin pouch from a hook on the wall and looped it over his shoulders. Kirra could hear something rattling around in there. "Let's go."

After shoveling in a few mouthfuls of stew, Kirra followed Luwan out of the hut and through several trees. He was working his way toward the ground, which was a little odd. Luwan usually liked to stay as high up as possible. She could tell he was moving more slowly than normal, certainly slower than when he was with his friends. Luwan was polite about letting Kirra go at her own pace. He knew she was doing the best she could.

When they were down to where only a few layers of branches separated them from the forest floor, he stopped. "This looks perfect," Luwan said. "I tried to pick a spot where the trees were packed pretty closely together. That should make it easier." He looked down and took a deep breath. "I hope."

Kirra looked around, wrinkling her brow. "Aren't we getting close to the river?" She cocked her head to listen for the telltale sign of the current, even though it would be more sluggish now with the lack of rain. "You're not trying to trick me into looking at that stupid raft, are you?"

"No! I promise. I just wanted to show you something."

"Does this have anything to do with what you're planning to ask your parents today?"

"It does." He sat down on a thick branch, took the pouch off his back, and set it on his lap. "Check these out." He pulled out two short, slender poles. They had been rounded into smooth curves at one end and had a loop of leather attached near the base.

"Wait, are those—?"

"Yes! Teeha helped me make them. Aren't they great?" He proudly held up one in each hand and shook them back and forth triumphantly.

"Okay, so . . . what are you going to do with them?"

"What do you mean? Isn't it obvious? I've decided what I want to do with my life. I'm going to join a group of Hook Hunters." He noticed the expression on Kirra's face. "What's the matter?"

"I don't know, Luwan, it's just . . . hook hunting is so risky. It's hard to imagine Loba being okay with this." Kirra knew that bringing up his father's reaction was partly an excuse. She would be worried about Luwan as well.

"That man has been telling me I have to *find my purpose* ever since I learned to walk. Well, I've found it. And he's just going to have to be okay with it." Luwan held her gaze, looking a little wounded. "Parents react negatively to everything the first time they hear about it. I expected you to be happy for me, Kirra."

"I'm sorry," she said with a sigh. Even though it made her uncomfortable, she had to admit it was the perfect job for Luwan. And if he could get all his energy out during the day on the hunt, maybe he would be a little calmer around the hut in the evenings.

If he made it back in the evening . . .

She pushed that thought aside. Luwan was going to do whatever Luwan decided to do, and Kirra could either choose to support him or not.

She nodded at the hooks in his hand. "So what's next? Do you have to practice with those things?" She had no idea what was involved in joining a Hook Hunter group.

"I already have been! Here, watch this."

Luwan stood and wrapped the leather straps around his wrists. Then he leaped to a neighboring branch, looping the hook on an overhead limb, and pull-stepped his way to another, and another. He started out a little shaky, tentative, but as he traced a wide circle around the spot where Kirra remained sitting, moving from tree to tree to tree, she could tell he was becoming more confident. His speed was nowhere near that of the actual Hook Hunters, but it was clear he had potential. Luwan was athletic and a natural daredevil; now he needed to develop fluidity. He made a few more passes around her, gaining speed as he went.

"Aren't you supposed to be quieter?" Kirra called to him.

"I don't think Hook Hunters do all that gasping and giggling. Kind of scares away the prey."

"I can't help it!" he called back. "This is so much fun!"

He must have heeded her advice, though, because he wiped the grin off his face and became silent and more intent as he continued to hook-jump-pull-lunge his way through the air.

Kirra leaned back and rested against the trunk, settling in for the show. Luwan would probably want to do this all morning. As he zoomed around and around the motion became hypnotic, and Kirra could feel herself being lulled almost to sleep.

That is, until one of Luwan's hooks either failed to gain purchase or he selected a bad branch. Either way, he lost his balance. Kirra leaned forward and put her hands over her mouth as he crashed through the screen of branches, snapping and cracking them noisily until he ended up in a heap on the forest floor.

At first, Kirra was frozen to the spot. She had never seen Luwan fall before, not once in all the years she had known him. It was scary and unsettling. And was there something else? A memory of another boy falling from a tree . . . ? She pushed that thought away almost before she knew it had surfaced.

Kirra could hardly breathe as she watched Luwan lying there, silently willing him to move, to get up.

Finally Luwan pushed himself into a sitting position, brushing leaves from his hair. He felt himself all over, head and ribs and legs, and seemed to determine that he was all right. Kirra felt like she could breathe again.

That's when she heard people calling to each other. Men, perhaps four or five different voices. Deep, gruff tones.

And she realized that she didn't understand the words.

Luwan tilted his head, listening. He had clearly heard them as well. Kirra, eyes wide, frantically motioned for him to get up and join her in the tree.

He popped to his feet and dashed for the trunk, perhaps limping a bit. When he got there, he scrambled up the tree until he was sitting on the limb next to her. He started to whisper something, but Kirra shook her head fiercely and placed a finger over her lips.

The two watched the forest together, and tromping through the brush came a half-dozen men, burdened by their spoils. One man had a forest buck slung around his neck, its two front hooves clasped in his right hand and the hind hooves in his left. Its throat had been slit to drain the blood and its head lolled to the side, eyes blank. Another man carried a length of rope in each hand, three fat guinea fowl dangling from both. Two other men supported a thick branch between them on their shoulders, the body of a leopard hanging from the middle.

They stopped where Luwan had fallen, pointing at the

branches that had dropped to the ground, then looked up at the surrounding trees. Kirra and Luwan stayed very still, trusting their dull-green-and-brown forest camouflage clothing to keep them hidden. They watched as the men spoke to each other in more of those words that Kirra did not understand but at the same time found horribly familiar.

Kirra could hardly think about their words or the forest animals they were holding. She had eyes only for their appearance. The skeletal arms attached to tall and powerful bodies. Leathery gray skin. Each man with a shock of white hair. The clothes made from leather and some kind of hard, shiny material. And the slender, cruel weapons belted to their waists.

The Takers had come to the Tree Folk.

15

KIRRA REMEMBERED EVERYTHING. All of it. All at once.

The volcano and little Tiko and storytelling contests and all the villages she had visited and her parents her real parents and that horrible camp and fire and smoke and . . .

Seeing those Takers, standing in the middle of her new home, was the Memory Trap she could not avoid. It grabbed her in a searingly painful grip and shook all the memories out of their carefully stored boxes.

And, oh, dear gods, how was her heart supposed to contain them all? How much more could she take before it burst?

16

SHE WASN'T TOUCHING THE GROUND. Her body bounced along. At first, she thought she might be floating but then understood that this boy was carrying her. A canopy of branches rushed by overhead.

He stopped at a tree, a particular tree, the same tree as before. Again, he craned his neck to look skyward and called to his parents for help. Just as he had done the first time.

Kirra was sitting on the floor, slumped against the wall for support. She could see the interior of the hut, but it was like she was viewing it at the end of a tunnel. She also couldn't tell if it was a picture from her memory or if she was really looking at it right now. It seemed like her eyes might be open but it was hard to tell. She couldn't move her head to look around, or at least she didn't want to. It felt like too monumental a task to undertake.

She could hear voices. They might have been inside the hut, but they were muffled, so maybe they were outside? Investigating this seemed much too difficult, and it didn't really matter, anyway.

Loba: . . . like she's here but not really here. She's acting like she did when she first arrived. What was that, four years ago now?

Maham: Oh, the poor thing. What happened?

Loba: She's never told us what happened before. What makes you think this time will be any different?

Maham: I was talking to Luwan.

Loba: Well, good, because it's no use talking to her. The first time, it took her weeks to snap out of this. Months, maybe.

Maham: And since then she has become our daughter. She's a hard worker and a good girl. Kirra has earned her place in this home, and you know it.

Loba: (A pause.) She has. I freely admit that. But what if

it takes her weeks to get well again? Who will tend to her this time? Luwan is older now, with responsibilities of his own, and much has to be done before—

Maham: It will take as long as it takes, and we will all tend to her, and that is that. Now, Luwan, tell us what happened. All of it.

Luwan: I already told you. We were just tree-walking near the ground to meet up with some of my friends, and we saw a group of hunters.

Maham: Why would a group of hunters make her react like this?

Luwan: They must have been from someplace far away, because—

Hunters.

The word caused Kirra to jolt upright. The back of her head hit the wall. The tunnel disappeared and the entire hut rushed to fill her field of vision, the light much too bright. And there was the family, huddled together and staring at her.

"Kirra?" Luwan bent down, looked into her eyes. "Are you feeling okay?"

"Hunters, no." She shook her head fiercely. "Not normal hunters. *Takers.*"

Maham dropped to one knee and rested a warm hand on Kirra's shoulder. "It's okay to be spooked. I understand that seeing people from distant lands can be unsettling." She rubbed Kirra's arm reassuringly. "But it's okay. This happens occasionally. We're completely hidden up here. All will be well."

"Yeah," Luwan said. "I tried to tell you. They're probably only on this side because the river is so low. After the rainy season comes, they'll stay on their side and not come back. You'll see."

Kirra opened her mouth to protest, but Loba stepped forward and spoke first. "Were you by the river, then? Taking her down there—in defiance of my orders—to jump on your foolish raft?"

"No, Father, I swear. We were just tree-walking, playing around."

Loba turned his gaze to Kirra. "Is this true?"

"Yes, but—" She shook her head. The raft didn't matter. Loba was focusing on the wrong thing.

"These hunters—Takers. Will not stay away. Will not stay on their side. They don't have sides. They think everything is their side." She rushed on, felt like she couldn't get the words out fast enough. "When they see what's here, they will come back. They'll take everything, until it's all gone. They'll take you. Us. Everyone. Everything."

"Wait." Loba gave her an intense look. "This is the way you talked when we first met you. Does this . . . ?" He glanced at Maham and Luwan before turning back to her. He lowered his voice. "Does this have anything to do with before? Before you came here?"

Kirra's eyes roved their curious faces. These people who had saved her life, cared for her, taken her into their family.

It had been incredibly gracious of them . . . But what would they have done if they had known the truth then?

What would they do with her if they found out now?

How could she possibly tell them she was responsible for destroying an entire community? That *she* was the reason everyone she had ever known and loved was . . .

The answer was easy. She couldn't tell them. She would never tell anybody.

But what would have happened if the Takers had seen her again this time? Followed her back to this tree?

As Kirra watched their faces, so familiar now, and so kind, she had a vision: This hut, these people, this tree, this entire forest, going up in flames as the black smoke choked her and she realized it was all her fault.

The darkness took her again.

Someone had put her in the hammock.

The next several days—or was it weeks?—passed by in a

haze as she lay there. Intense memories rose up, one after the other, so many of them that her mind would black out to prevent a fatal overload. But ultimately that was no help at all, because in the darkness of sleep the dreams would come, visions of what must have taken place in the volcano. And then her body would jolt awake to save her from the horror of the dreams. And so the cycle continued. It was impossible to say which was worse—waking or dreaming—and most of the time she couldn't figure out which was which.

Interspersed with this unyielding terror were blips of relief. She was barely aware of what was happening, but she tried to hold on to these moments. Luwan bringing her a cup of water and helping her sip. Maham lying in the next hammock and pressing a cool strip of cloth to her forehead. Loba trying to entice her with a freshly grilled strip of crocodile meat. These acts of compassion saved her from being completely sucked into the black storm raging inside her mind.

One morning, Kirra opened her eyes to birdsong and a breeze rustling the leaves. She was mentally and emotionally exhausted, but the flood of memories had slowed to a trickle. The rest of them were still lurking, she was quite certain, ready to overflow and engulf her at any time. But at least for this moment, her mind was mostly clear. Functional, anyway.

Kirra took the opportunity to think about what she should do next.

She could brush off Loba's questions, pretend everything was fine, agree with the family that this was just a random group of hunters and they would wander back to their own land soon, never to be heard from again. But she knew she would never do this. For one thing, this family had been much too good to her, and for another thing, lying and pretending were not going to keep the Takers from coming back.

Another option was confessing everything, of course. That was also not something she'd be able to do. After losing one family . . . could she really look another family in their eyes and watch their faces as tolerance toward her turned to doubt and anger and revulsion and hate? She did not think she could survive that.

When the true answer came to her, it was so simple she was honestly shocked that it had taken so long.

She must leave. Now. And never come back.

The fall of Zedu had been her fault. Entirely. But it was everyone else in her native community who had suffered. And what had happened to her? She was living comfortably with nice people, safely hidden in the trees with plenty to eat.

She didn't deserve this—some part of her had always

known this—and the gods would not allow it. *That* was why the Takers had shown up. It was her inescapable punishment, coming to find her at last.

If she left, the Tree Folk would be spared.

She should have made the ultimate sacrifice at the Takers' camp that night, presented herself to Red Streak and his troops and accepted the outcome as a consequence of sneaking Outside without her father. If she'd only had the courage to do that back then, Zedu would still be a happy and thriving community today.

But instead she had run, taken the easy way out, and ended up leading the Takers right to Zedu's doorstep.

So now it was time for her to accept the fate she had rightfully earned. Exile herself from her second home, and keep the Tree Folk safe.

Kirra listened carefully for any sounds coming from the hut above. All was silent. The family must be out and about their business in the forest. Perfect.

She pulled herself out of her hammock and made her way to the platform above. It would take a quick minute to pack her few possessions and then she could leave this place forever.

17

THE POUCH ON KIRRA'S BACK was relatively light. It hadn't felt right to take any food from the family for her journey, even though she had caught or prepared much of it herself, so she only had her clothing and a cutting stone. It would be enough. It was more than she deserved.

She hesitated, toes on the edge of the circular platform that surrounded the hut. As usual, she paused for a moment out of nervousness and respect for the two-hundred-foot drop to the ground. Kirra lingered even longer this time, heartbroken at the thought of never seeing these people again, never getting to—

She pushed those thoughts away. They would paralyze her. She was going to have to get better at avoiding Memory Traps. She'd have a double set of them now—one for each home she had lost.

As she stood there, she detected a faint scent drifting into the forest. She raised her nose and sniffed: It was the fresh smell of moisture gathering in the air. Kirra shaded her eyes with her hand and looked to the east, where billowy clouds had started to form and appeared to be headed this direction. The wet season was finally on its way. Maybe not today, but soon.

She sighed. Having to contend with heavy rains didn't make her decision to leave any easier. It would be more difficult to find food and nearly impossible to build a dry shelter. But, she admitted to herself, there was never going to be a good time. She just had to do it.

Kirra took a deep breath and extended one leg out over the open air. As soon as her foot hit the branch, she heard a voice say, "Where do you think you're going?"

She flinched and glanced up. Luwan was perched on a branch above the hut. As she looked at him, his friends started to emerge from behind the surrounding screen of leaves. There was Teeha, the builder, with her rough hands and serious face. Kharee, a muscular boy a few years older than her, along with his younger brother, Mozan. And finally, Makina, a small but agile girl who could zip through the trees almost faster than a Hook Hunter.

Invisible to Kirra just a moment before, they suddenly appeared, as if parts of the tree had come to life.

They all stepped easily onto the platform. She just stared at them, heart racing.

"It's so good to see you out of the hammock!" Luwan said. "You feeling better?"

She nodded.

"So." He gestured to the pouch on her back. "Where are you headed?"

Kirra cleared her throat. "Oh . . . you know. I have to try to get to the salt caverns. I need to repay Mome for his loan."

"Is that right?" Luwan took a few steps toward her. "Then what's in the pouch? Shouldn't it be empty?"

"Oh . . . I borrowed some other things from him as well. I need to return them."

Kharee scoffed and shook his head.

Mozan whispered, "She's not a very good liar."

Makina clapped a hand over her mouth to stifle a giggle at that.

Luwan stepped closer and reached for the pouch. Kirra didn't move to stop him. She felt as if she had no fight left in her. He gently grabbed the strings and lifted the little knapsack off her shoulders, then opened it up and looked through the contents.

"These are all your clothes," Luwan said. He looked back up at her with soft, sad eyes. "Please tell me that you aren't trying to leave."

"You don't understand—I have to." She snatched the pouch back from him. In her desperation to get away, her words tumbled out in a rush. "I know you won't be able to understand, even though you'll try, because you're a good person, but please don't get in my way, because if I don't leave right now, then something very bad could—"

"Shh." Luwan took her by the shoulders. "Just listen to me for a minute, all right?"

She shook off his hands, looked at the ground. "Luwan, please, I can't—"

"Hey, it's me. You can trust me." Luwan looked at her steadily until she raised her head and met his gaze. "We have something to show you."

Kirra scanned his friends' faces. All of them were offering her sympathetic smiles—except Teeha, who never smiled at anyone.

"Now listen," Luwan said softly. "If I say the word *hunters*"—he whispered it—"you're not going to lose it again, are you?"

Kirra took a deep breath and then shook her head.

"Good." Luwan smiled, too. "Because I think we might have solved that particular problem."

The river's current was lazy, but Kirra could still hear it. She had been traveling for a while through the trees with Luwan and his friends, and now her breathing started to become shallow and she could feel her hands getting clammy as she realized they were approaching the place where the group of Takers had been spotted.

"Why are you bringing me back here?"

Luwan turned and grinned at her. "You'll see. Just another minute." He hopped to a lower branch, and another, and then scrambled all the way down the trunk until he was standing on the ground. He looked up and waved for Kirra to join him, and the rest of his friends followed.

Luwan led the little band around a copse of trees and then the river was before them. Kirra's heart started thundering at the sight, but she clenched her fists and took deep breaths. She needed to keep it together, stop being so fragile and pitiful. And, though she didn't believe for a moment that Luwan and his friends had solved anything, she owed it to him to at least see what they wanted to show her.

"We've been spying on them. The hunters," Luwan said. He pointed downriver. "Do you see what they've built to get back and forth? It's very clever."

Kirra squinted. On the riverbank there was a wooden post with a rope looped around it. The rope stretched across the water and was tied to a corresponding post on the opposite side. Resting by the post on the far shore was a raft that was tethered to the rope. *So,* she thought, *after the Takers finish their raids, they must use this contraption to ferry their game back and forth.*

Kirra's mind raced. The good news was that they were taking their plunder *away* from the Tree Folk, back to the other side of the river. The bad news was that Kirra knew they wouldn't stop there. When more of them realized how good the hunting was over here, more of them would show up. And even if they didn't decimate the entire animal population of the forest, they were bound to discover the homes in the trees eventually. And then another community of good people would be destroyed.

"Hey. You still with us?" Luwan shook her gently by the shoulder, jostling her out of her thoughts.

She nodded.

"Okay," he said. "They went hunting three times last week. But we haven't seen them in several days."

Makina stepped forward. "The rains will be coming any day now, but we think they're going to try at least one more time, since they've left that raft there."

Mozan added, "After the river rises, their pulley system will be worthless. No way it will work."

"We're going to be ready for them," Luwan said. "And we're going to make sure they never come back."

"No." Kirra shook her head. "Don't do anything to them. Please. *Stay away from them.*" Her eyes pleaded with Luwan and she grabbed his arms with both hands. "You don't understand. The best thing you can do is hide. Remain safe up in the trees." Kirra felt a frantic desire to leave. The longer she stayed here, the more danger these people were in. She had to get on with her punishment and exile herself to keep the Takers away.

"Shh." Luwan broke her grip lightly and turned her desperate clutching at him into an embrace. He held her for a few moments until her shaking subsided. "Come on, Kirra. At least let us show you what we've built."

"You've built something?" She pulled back and gave him a look. "What do you mean?"

"Luwan—he told us." Kharee stepped forward. "These hunters, they scared you. We wanted to scare them back."

Luwan grinned. "My friend Kharee doesn't always have the best way with words, but that pretty much sums it up."

Kirra shook her head. "But you can't scare these—"

"Yes we can!" Little Makina marched right up to her, the girl's head barely reaching Kirra's waist. She talked as fast as she moved through the trees. "We were all talking about it, and when we spied on the hunters, we saw how big they were, and I said, 'They look like giants,' but I didn't think anybody would listen, because everyone looks like a giant to me, practically, but then Mozan agreed with me, which is funny, because he never agrees with me about anything, and Kharee also agreed with me, which is even funnier, because he's pretty gigantic himself, and that's when I said I wish we could be giants, too, because then they would be as scared of us as you were scared of them, and then Teeha joined in the conversation, which is weird, because she doesn't say much, you know, but she said, 'What if we actually *could* be giants?' and then she and Luwan went away and talked and came up with their plan and then came back and told us and we all liked it, and then we worked really hard the whole time you were in your hammock, and Teeha is a really good builder and we are really good helpers—me, especially—and now we want to show it to you, because Luwan thinks it might help you smile and be yourself again, so will you let us show you now? Please?"

Kirra peered around at all the faces gazing eagerly at her. Had they really made this whatever-it-was for *her*? No—it had been for Luwan, really. But *he* had wanted to do it for her, and the rest of them seemed to want to make both of them happy.

She reached down and tousled Makina's hair. "Well, I don't see how I can say no to all that."

Makina clapped and hugged Kirra fiercely, then grabbed her by the hand and tugged her deeper into the forest. "Come on, it's right up here." She led Kirra and the others to the ferry post the Takers had set up on this side of the river, then started to follow a path that led into the forest.

As the band of friends walked along, Kirra turned to Luwan, raising her eyebrows at him in a question.

Luwan gestured to indicate the path they were walking on. "This is the access point for the hunters. They come this way every time—saves them from having to clear a new trail for each hunt." He pointed up ahead. "They split up eventually, in ones or twos, to cover more ground and get more game, but at this spot they are always still together. And so they will all see *this* at the same time." Luwan spread his arms wide with a flourish.

Kirra looked up. And, oh, by the gods, what had they done?

Towering over their heads, a good twenty feet above the forest floor, a great face emerged from a screen of leaves and stared down at them. The face alone was as tall as Makina, and it was scowling at them with thick, furrowed brows and a long, sharp nose.

Kirra stepped back, her hand over her chest. Luwan laughed and clapped her on the shoulder. "Doesn't it look real? I told you, Teeha is amazing. She can build anything."

Teeha crossed her arms over her chest and nodded her agreement with this assessment.

As Kirra looked closer, she could see the illusion for what it was: a huge structure made of wood and mud and rocks and brush. But still. It had looked real enough when she first glanced up at it. A forest giant, just like something out of a story.

"It's pretty incredible," Kirra breathed.

Makina tugged on her arm. "I made the nose all by myself," she whispered. "Well, mostly."

"You did a nice job. That thing is hideous."

Makina beamed.

Kirra stepped back a few paces to take in the entire scene. The face was impressive, but she realized that wasn't even half of it. In between the leaves she could see two thick arms descending, so long that the knuckles almost dragged on the ground, and also two sturdy legs that had been crafted out of fallen logs. Draped around these limbs were old quilts, pieces of clothing, and strips of fabric that had all been sewn together, so it appeared as if the huge creature were wearing a tattered multicolored cloak.

Kirra had to admit that the whole thing really did look like a giant lurking among the leafy trees.

"Teeha showed us how to build the skeleton out of wood," Luwan said, "and then use the trees to prop it up, anchor the whole thing in place."

"The trees are the real giants," Mozan said. "They're just helping us with our fake giant."

"And then, as you can see, we filled it in with anything we could find in the forests," Luwan said. "We didn't have time to make a body, but we think it's still going to be enough. It doesn't have to be perfect—if all goes well, they won't be getting close enough to examine it—but just good enough to work one time."

Kirra wrinkled her brow in confusion. "Good enough to work how?"

"To scare them away!" Makina said.

Kirra studied the entire structure. She cleared her throat. "It's good, really good—Teeha, the craftsmanship is incredible, and I have no idea how you all pulled this off . . . but do you really think they're going to be afraid of it?"

"Oh, it gets even better." Luwan grinned. "Teeha also knows all about mechanics—straps and hinges and ropes and pulleys and levers. She even snuck down and studied the ferry rig that the hunters put together to get ideas about how to make it move. Isn't that just perfect? We all tried to—"

"Wait—it *moves*?" Kirra said.

"Yes!" Makina shouted. "Teeha, tell her how you got the idea!"

The stoic builder shrugged and looked at the ground, clearly uncomfortable with all the attention. "It was nothing. I just . . . I remembered these puppets that my dad made for me when I was a little girl. The head and arms and legs were all connected to strings, and you could hold a little board where the strings were attached, and when you moved the board this way and that, you could make the doll move around. Dance or walk or whatever."

Kirra nodded. "I had one of those when I was little, too."

"Uh, everybody?" Kharee said. "We need to show Kirra how it moves. Now."

"We will," Luwan said. "Just first let us—"

"No," Kharee said. "Now." He pointed across the water.

The group of Takers was making its way across the river stones on the opposite shore, heading for their raft.

18

"GET TO YOUR STATIONS!" Luwan cried.

The rest of the gang scurried about, scrambling up trees and placing themselves at various positions around the huge puppet. Luwan grabbed Kirra's hand and pulled her into the forest.

They climbed a tree above and behind the giant's head so Kirra could peek through the leaves and have a good view of what was happening below. When he found the perfect vantage point, Luwan took Kirra by the shoulders and slowly lowered her to a seat on a wide branch. He bent over and peered into her eyes. "Look, I know this is scary for you. I don't pretend to understand or know why—because you have never told me anything about, you know, before you came here—but I trust you. I believe you have a good reason to be afraid of these hunters, okay?"

Kirra nodded, grateful he wasn't pressing her for more information.

"So please trust *me*. We've been practicing all week, while you've been . . . resting. So even though I know these men spook you, will you be able to stay while they approach? Watch what happens?"

She looked past him, saw that the Takers were already halfway across the river, the whole crew pulling hand over hand to ferry the raft across the sluggish but steady current. Digging her fingernails into the branch she was sitting on, she took a deep breath. "I will."

He leaned in and gave her a big hug. "I'm proud of you."

Proud of her for what? Not fainting? She clenched her teeth in frustration at her helplessness but managed to say, "Good luck, Luwan. And please be safe. I'll be worried about you."

He waggled his eyebrows at her. "Those hunters are the ones who have to worry."

Luwan turned and hopped down a few branches until he was directly behind the mouth of the giant puppet. He looked around at everyone else already at their stations, exchanging nods and silent signals of encouragement. They were ready.

Within a few minutes, the half-dozen Takers sauntered along the path and into the little clearing before the tree, dressed in that clothing designed to protect them from anything—beast or man or natural disaster—they might ever encounter. It took an act of fierce willpower for Kirra to remain in her seat, silently watching. The urge to run away was overwhelming.

Luwan took a horn hanging from his belt and held it up to his lips. At the same time, his foot found a lever connected to the lower jaw of the puppet. As he pumped his leg on the lever, the puppet's enormous mouth clattered open and closed. "RAAWWRR!" Magnified and distorted by the horn, Luwan's voice was gruff and powerful, the roar of a demon.

The Takers' reaction would have been comical if Kirra hadn't been so terrified. All of their heads snapped up as one, and they stumbled backward, reaching out and holding on to one another for support so they didn't topple over. That worked for almost all of them. One Taker was sent tumbling to land awkwardly on his ample backside.

As he scrambled to his feet, that Taker and all the others withdrew those long weapons from the coverings that were belted to their waists, flicking them open to expose the slender silver blades. "Who . . . who goes there?" one of the

Takers called out. Kirra noticed these interlopers had gotten better at learning the language of this land over the last four years, but that didn't help the delivery. Perhaps it was wishful thinking on Kirra's part, but for someone who was supposed to be the leader of this group, his voice certainly sounded shaky.

"I PROTECT THE FOREST!" Luwan boomed. He turned and gave a signal to Mozan, who pulled on a series of ropes. This caused the puppet to lift one gigantic arm, slowly curl his branch-fingers into a fist, and shake it back and forth at the Takers.

The hunters glanced at one another uneasily, dismay and perhaps the beginnings of fear showing on their long gray faces. A few of them motioned to the one who had spoken up. They pushed him forward.

He took a few halting steps into the clearing, raising his right arm, and pointed his sharp weapon up at the puppet. In her memories of that terrible night in the encampment, that weapon had been impossibly long and cruel, but today it looked puny and pathetic in comparison to the great forest giant.

Luwan signaled to Kharee and Teeha below. They leaped up to grab overhead ropes, let their weight drop them to the ground, and then released the ropes. They jumped up again and again, allowing the ropes to lower them back to the forest floor before letting go. This caused the puppet's enormous log legs, wrapped in cloth, to rise and fall heavily, pounding the dirt with a great thud each time. Kirra could feel the tremors as the sound shook the tree she was sitting in. She also noticed that the Takers all took a few steps backward.

"LEAVE THIS PLACE!" Luwan boomed. He worked his foot double time on the lever, making that huge mouth clack open and closed angrily.

Down on the ground, the leader motioned to one of the other hunters, who reached up and grabbed something slung over his shoulder. It looked like a bow, but it was held horizontally instead of vertically. The man fitted it with an arrow and then worked some sort of a handle in a circular motion. The man then leveled the weapon on his shoulder, took aim, and the arrow came whizzing straight at them.

In reflex, Kirra put her hands over her head and ducked. But the arrow merely stuck into the wood of the huge puppet's face.

Luwan signaled to Teeha and Kharee below, who scrambled up the tree trunk. Mohan furiously worked at his ropes, and the giant's arm bent backward until it disappeared through the screen of leaves.

Kharee and Teeha grabbed a big rock, roughly the size of a half-grown pig, that had been stashed in the crook of a tree branch. They each put both arms under and strained to lift it.

While they were doing that, Mozan worked a lever that brought the arm back farther and farther, and Makina came over to cinch it tight with a length of rope. When Kharee and Teeha set the rock into the puppet's branch fingers, Kirra finally figured out what they were doing.

The giant's wooden arm had been designed to throw! Like a weapon she had heard about in stories from long ago—a catapult.

Mozan removed a slender cutting stone from his belt and whacked at the rope, severing it in one blow. The arm exploded forward, ripping through the leaves and launching the big rock into the air.

It happened so fast, the Takers didn't have time to scatter. The rock sailed across the clearing and smashed down on the foot of the hunter who had shot the arrow.

"Aaahhh!" His howl of pain tore through the forest. The man desperately tried to move, to run away, but his foot was pinned to the earth. He turned his head and spat an unintelligible stream of words at the five men cowering in fear behind him. Kirra was willing to bet that some of those were curses.

Keeping their wide eyes trained on the giant lest he attack again, the Takers dashed forward as a group. Three of them extended their weapons toward the menace in front of them, while two others lifted the stone off their fellow hunter. His anguished screams of pain only increased. As two men put his arms around their shoulders to carry him out, Luwan had his friends draw the giant's arm back again. This time they filled the wooden grip with smaller rocks and sticker balls from the thorny bushes.

"NEVER RETURN!" The catapult arm whooshed forward, and the retreating Takers were pelted with a shower of hard, sharp missiles. They cried out in pain and increased their pace, hustling to get back to their ferry.

The kids in the tree waited breathlessly, watching from behind the leaves as the hunters made it to the raft, spilling weapons and the injured man clumsily onto the wooden surface. Luwan's crew stifled giggles as the man cried out in pain and anger at his hunting mates. It wasn't until the raft had made it to the other side, well out of earshot, that Luwan and his friends allowed themselves to cheer and hug and clap one another on the back.

"You see?" Luwan looked up at Kirra, beaming. "I don't think we have to worry about seeing those Takers around here ever again!"

19

". . . GET A LOOK AT HIS FACE? I've never seen anything like . . ."

". . . didn't know eyes could even get that wide! He must . . ."

". . . that thing that shot the arrow? I need one of those to . . ."

". . . so great when he fell down, and the other guys didn't even . . ."

The entire crew was lounging on the banks of the river,

talking over one another, telling war stories about success-fully using the giant puppet to scare away the hunters.

Kirra sat a little apart from the rest, keeping her thoughts to herself. They had worked so hard and deserved to laugh and celebrate. And she had certainly experienced a rush of euphoria as she'd watched the Takers turn tail and stumble away, racing to get back to the other side of the river to dis-appear into the brush.

But still, she couldn't stop worrying about what would come next. Was it possible that the forest giant would be enough of a deterrent, a frightening-enough threat to keep the Takers away for good? The illusion was clever and well constructed, and she had no doubt that the archer's smashed toes would make him reluctant to return. But as grateful as she was to Luwan and his friends for doing all this, she couldn't help but think the men must have realized it was a decoy of some kind . . . or a youngster's prank.

The best she could hope for was that the hunters would be too embarrassed to tell their comrades about what hap-pened, but they would steer them in another direction. On the other hand, if the Takers never heard about it, then all this had been for nothing.

Kirra sighed. She'd had such clarity of purpose upon waking up this morning—her leaving would save the Tree Folk from the Takers. Even though she'd been heartbroken at the prospect of going away, at least she'd had a clear direction set in her mind. Now she wasn't sure what would be the best thing to do, and the uncertainty was almost worse than the sadness.

After an hour or so of imaginative reminiscing, the confrontation growing bigger and more legendary with each retelling, the group wore itself out. Luwan and his friends lolled back against the riverbank, hands clasped behind their heads as they gazed up at the sky.

"Look at those clouds," Mozan said. "Finally. You think the rain will start tonight?"

"Tomorrow at the latest," Kharee said.

"Those hunters are going to be soaked unless they can get back to wherever they came from, and fast."

Luwan laughed. "Did you see how quickly they were trying to escape the great and mighty forest giant? They must be miles away by now."

Kirra hoped so.

The group went back to studying the sky. After a while, Makina spoke up. "This is the longest dry spell I can ever remember in my entire life."

"Your entire life? What are you, about five years old?" Luwan sniggered. "I'm sorry to say, Makina, but the span of your living memory is not all that impressive." The others joined him in laughter.

"I'm twelve! Well, almost. And I can't help it if I'm small for my age," Makina huffed. "And besides, my parents said the same thing. They say it could be the longest dry season ever of all time."

"Oh, quit picking on her, Luwan," Teeha said.

The group quieted down again. Kirra watched as Makina sat up and sneered at the boys, then looked back and forth from the river to her friends.

"Hey, Luwan," she finally said. "You're always talking about how you're going to cross over to the other side someday. Why not now?"

Luwan sat up and studied the river. "Nah. I'll do it some other time."

Makina pressed on. "But the river might never be this low again. This could be your last chance this season."

Luwan cupped his chin in his hand, looked out across the meandering current.

Kirra had to speak up. "Oh, Luwan. Please don't tell me you're actually considering this."

Makina shrugged. "Maybe he's just afraid. How old are you, anyway, Luwan? *Five?*"

Luwan, still full of himself from the victory over the Takers, puffed out his chest. "I'm nearly full grown. I could do it right now, no problem."

"I bet you couldn't get across and just touch a single tree on the other side."

"Stop it, Makina." Teeha shook her head. "I agree with Kirra. Don't do this, Luwan. There's no need."

Luwan jumped to his feet. "You know what? Sometimes you don't need a reason to do something amazing!" he cried, and ran full tilt toward the river.

Kirra gasped and put her hand over her chest. Her first instinct was to jump up and run after him, grab him, and drag him back to the safety of their little group. But she knew that was useless. As always, Luwan was going to do what Luwan was going to do.

So all she could do was sit there and watch as he splashed into the river and started chugging forward, first in water up to his knees, then his waist, and finally his chest. When it got almost to his shoulders, Kirra could tell he was struggling to keep his footing.

"That boy is crazy sometimes." Kharee shook his head.

Teeha scoffed. "That boy is stupid sometimes."

Kirra watched in silence as Luwan got smaller with distance, his head bobbing up and down as if he were jumping off the riverbed to keep himself above the surface. Out in the middle, it must have been so deep that he couldn't touch at all, because he started swimming, pumping his arms and legs furiously as the current pushed him downstream.

Kirra hadn't realized she'd been holding her breath until Luwan finally got past the middle, close enough to the other side that his feet had found the bottom once more and he was straining forward, wading until the water was back down to his chest, his waist, and finally his ankles. Kirra could start breathing again.

When Luwan strode out of the river, safely on the other side, he turned and raised his arms in triumph. His friends stood and applauded him, whistling and cheering.

Makina cupped her hands around her mouth and shouted, "Remember! You have to touch at least one tree!"

The forest over there was sparser, a collection of stunted trees and scraggly brush. Kirra wasn't sure if Luwan could hear Makina or not, but in any case, he ran up the river-bank, slapped a tree, and turned back to the group to raise his hands again, a huge smile on his face as he reveled in his accomplishment.

That's when two monstrous men, clad in leather, dashed out from behind the tree line, grabbed Luwan roughly by each arm, and dragged him into the brush.

20

KIRRA'S CLARITY OF PURPOSE returned in an instant.

"Teeha!" She clutched the larger girl by the shoulders. "Take everyone to our hut, tell Loba and Maham what has happened. Tell them *everything*, understand? Don't leave anything out. The puppet, the river, all of it."

Teeha looked as wide-eyed and stunned as Kirra felt, but she just nodded once. "I can do that."

"But what are *you* going to do?" Makina wailed.

"This is my fault. I need to go and try to help him. Now."

Kharee and Mozan stepped forward, protests on their

lips, but Kirra turned her back on them and fled before they could speak. "Go! Now!" she called over her shoulder.

It felt maddening to be running in the opposite direction, away from Luwan. But she couldn't cross the river here. Those hunters must have been watching, lying in wait. She had to put some distance between her and the Takers, cross the river unnoticed, and then sneak back over on land to try and find them.

Kirra could not let panic seize control. The mind muscles she'd built up over the years in order to keep the Memory Traps at bay were helpful now. She was able to block out all other thoughts and maintain a sharp focus only on what needed to be done: get across the water undetected, find Luwan, bring him home.

Running was a slog, her feet either sinking into soft sand or tripping over stones. But she kept her eyes trained on the bend in the river ahead. If she could get around that, she would be shielded from the Takers' view. Kirra was also careful to head upstream, knowing that the current would push her sideways, as it had Luwan. She wanted to be carried closer to the spot where they had nabbed Luwan, not farther away.

Finally, she reached the bend and raced the length of the curved riverbank. Glancing behind her to make sure she was out of the field of vision of whoever might be close to where

Luwan had been taken, she turned and plunged into the river.

Luwan was much taller than she, so the water was over her head sooner, but she just kept moving, churning her arms and legs, struggling inch by inch to get across. There was a moment of terror when the current seemed too strong, and the feeling of being overtaken by a powerful natural force washed over her again. Worse, some part of her thought there would be comfort in surrendering to the river, letting the current sweep her away from her life with the Tree Folk and all the problems she had caused. But she didn't give in this time. She kept fighting, and soon her feet were dragging along the riverbed and she could force one foot in front of the other until finally she was on all fours on the opposite bank, gasping for breath.

She stood up and scanned the countryside to get her bearings. Kirra glanced back at the other side and realized the river had dragged her past the spot where she'd been sitting with Luwan and his friends.

That got her moving again. She didn't want to be spotted by the Takers before she could help Luwan.

Kirra pushed herself up and ran for the tree line, working her way inside the underbrush. Concealed by the foliage, she paused to wipe the water out of her eyes and get her bearings.

Her instinct was to move quickly, dash this way and that to find where they had taken Luwan. She guessed they had a camp nearby where they were bringing the game and dressing it, perhaps smoking it all so they could carry a big load of meat back to the main group.

But she realized that, as difficult as it might be, she needed to prioritize stealth over speed. So she walked carefully, slowly, to avoid making noise, keeping one ear cocked to the sounds of the forest, listening for clues.

Just like the first time she'd set out in search of a Takers' encampment, it was not difficult to locate them. Perhaps they had so much confidence in their special clothing and cruel weapons that they didn't think it necessary to take evasive measures. It seemed it was not in their nature to hide.

And even if they were out of sight, the smells would have drawn Kirra straight to them. The sweet and pungent odor of meat being smoked filled the air, getting stronger as she took each step.

Kirra made it to the space the Takers had cleared out for their camp and she crouched behind a thicket of brush to observe. A couple of crude lean-tos had been slapped together for shelter, and several fire pits were set up to facilitate the meat smoking, flames roaring at each one.

A group of six Takers was huddled up in the middle of the clearing having a heated discussion, making broad gestures with those eerily long arms. About what to do with Luwan, she had no doubt.

And there he was, the boy who had saved her life all those years ago. The person who had given her a family when she didn't deserve one. Sitting on the ground, his wrists and ankles tied together with rope.

The sight of him there, trussed up like a wild animal and completely helpless, at the mercy of these merciless men, made her feel like doing a dozen different things all at once: Cry. Scream. Collapse. But mostly take the cutting stone from where it was belted at her waist and charge into the middle of the clearing and gut them all.

Instead, she closed her eyes and took a deep breath. She had to keep it together in order to have any chance of rescuing him.

When her heart rate had calmed and she could think clearly again, she reopened her eyes and surveyed the scene. She needed to make a plan.

Unfortunately, the trees on this side of the river were no good for climbing. They were short and spindly and barely had any branches at all. Getting above the hunters and pulling off a surprise rescue, as she had done before, was not an option.

What else . . . ?

While the hunters were in the middle of their intense

meeting, she could sneak over and snatch some of the meat, then wade into the brush and try to use it to lure danger-ous animals into the camp. She would likely not have to go far to find a willing participant. And Kirra thought the Takers would be much less menacing if there were suddenly a couple of hungry leopards prowling around the middle of their site.

But that was no good. The leopards wouldn't know they were being used to save Luwan, and the tied-up piece of prey would probably seem like the best option for the big cats.

What if she could stall the men somehow? Make her presence known and then race off into the trees, lead them on a wild-goose chase? When Loba heard the news from Teeha and the others, he would surely come charging down here with his hunting weapons. Would she be able to keep the Takers distracted and Luwan safe until reinforcements arrived?

Or maybe she could—

One of the Takers broke away from the huddled group. He marched over to a cooking fire and pulled out a stick that had been halfway in the flames. The tip glowed an angry red.

This Taker then stalked over to Luwan.

"Tell us . . . about giant. Other side of river," he growled.

Luwan lifted his head and stared defiantly at the man. "He protects the forest."

The Taker took a step closer to Luwan. "How many giants?"

"Hundreds." Luwan smirked. "*Thousands*. They are everywhere. You should untie me now before they come to rescue me. They can cross the river in one step."

Several of the Takers glanced uneasily around the surrounding woods at that.

"Seriously," Luwan continued. "Leave this place now and never come back. Or they will get you."

"There are hundreds of giants?" The hunter pointed a long gray finger back in the direction of the Tree Folk community. Luwan nodded confidently.

The hunter took a step even closer. "Then why do they not harm your people?"

The defiant look drained from Luwan's face. He clearly had not prepared an answer for that question.

Another Taker stepped up beside the first one. "How many like you live in forest? How big is group?"

Kirra watched Luwan's eyes go wide as he figured out what they were after. He shook his head quickly and his voice became more frantic, shaky. "No big group. Just me and my friends. Passing through. Camping. We're on a journey."

The first Taker held up the stick and slowly extended it so that the red-hot ember at the tip was mere inches from Luwan's face. He turned his head away from it, but the second man stepped forward and grabbed Luwan by the throat to stifle his movement. Those fingers, so dry and dimply that they looked almost reptilian, dug into Luwan's flesh. Luwan made gagging sounds that curdled Kirra's blood.

"No lies," the second Taker snarled. "We know people are living in forest. We can feel them watching. They hide from us."

"But they do not try to be stopping us. Must be *weak*," said the first Taker, spitting the last word. "So tell us— NOW—how do your people protect from giant? Tell us!" the man shouted as he shoved the burning stick at Luwan, jabbing back and forth, nearly skewering him each time.

It was then that Kirra realized the big difference between this interrogation and the first one she'd seen with the Takers. Red Streak had been cruel but confident. Ultimately, he was in control of himself because he knew he was in control of the situation.

But these men? They were *scared*. It showed in their wide eyes and jittery movements and strained voices.

Scared people were much more dangerous. They were capable of anything.

"Tell us truth!"

Luwan just shook his head. The man bellowed in rage and lunged forward to press the fiery stick against Luwan's chest while his companion held down the boy. Kirra could hear it sizzle before Luwan's tortured scream tore through the forest and ripped right through Kirra's heart.

The stick was jerked away, revealing the angry welt that had been burned into Luwan's flesh.

"Tell us!"

The Taker lunged again. Another terrible scream. Another ugly welt.

He held the stick up to Luwan's face in a hand that was trembling with fear. "Next one—take out your eye," he growled.

That was it. Kirra grabbed the cutting stone from where it was belted at her waist and held it in a death grip. She was not going to lose another brother without a fight.

But as she started to stride into the clearing, come what may, the words flowed from Luwan in a rush.

"Okay, stop. Stop! I will tell you. The giant isn't real! We made him. My friends and I, we built him to scare you. It's not real. Please, stop. Just stop."

The Takers all froze and stared at one another. One of them shook his head in disgust and jerked a thumb at Luwan. "Kill him. We need to pack up before the rain starts."

"Wait." The one with the stick leaned in, glaring in Luwan's face. "The giant . . . Someone *made* that? How is that possible?"

"Ha!" one of the hunters from the huddled group cried.

He pointed at the man with the stick and laughed cruelly. A stream of that unfamiliar language came pouring from him, and although Kirra could not understand the words, they were being delivered in a mocking tone and the message was obvious: *I told you so.*

The hunter with the stick did not appreciate being laughed at. He strode over, flung the burning stick at the other man, and then got close enough to take a great swing with his meaty fist, connecting with the man's jaw with a *crunch.* And then the entire group was at one another, punching and kicking and swinging and gouging. Including the man who had been holding down Luwan.

This was Kirra's chance. She angled around thickets of brush, keeping herself concealed but working her way to a bush behind Luwan.

She was nearly there when one of the men—the leader who had emerged in the confrontation with the puppet— drew his weapon, held it over his head, and shouted a single word: "STOP!"

Kirra crouched behind a too-skinny tree and froze. At first, she thought he was talking to her, but then she realized he was bringing order back to his troop.

The leader spat angry words at the group of bruised and bleeding men, who grumbled and hung their heads but separated.

Then the man in charge approached Luwan. Kirra was

close enough to see tears in Luwan's eyes, and she knew they were as much about shame as they were about pain.

When the leader was in front of his captive he said, in a very matter-of-fact tone, "We will destroy your giant. Then destroy your people."

He withdrew a blade from his belt. Kirra braced herself to leap out swinging with her cutting stone, when the first fat raindrop fell with a splash on her nose.

More raindrops quickly followed, pattering the dry leaves on the ground. The hunters looked to the sky, then ducked their heads and covered themselves with blankets. In an instant, it became a downpour the likes of which Kirra had never seen, never even heard tales of. A great clap of thunder announced its arrival, and the storm built with astonishing speed. Soon it was like she was standing underneath a waterfall.

The forest floor turned into a web of rivulets and streams. The hunters cried out as the lean-tos collapsed and their gear started to wash away. They all scrambled around the camp, scooping up their stuff and frantically shouting orders.

Kirra raced to Luwan, gripped the soaking-wet rope, and hacked away at the knots that bound him. He simply sat there, stunned, and studied her through the sheets of rain.

Finally the ropes gave away and he was free. She tugged at his arm and he followed, stumbling at first but quickly regaining his agility. As they dashed away from the camp, they heard the hunters yelling at them. Screaming in rage. Kirra charged ahead, wading straight through the brush instead of taking the time to try and find a path, thorns tearing at her skin.

Kirra glanced behind them and saw they were being pursued by all six of the Takers, the big men slashing at the thicket with their long weapons as they trudged toward them.

She pulled Luwan and they hurried onward, twisting this way and that around trees and thick patches of underbrush, but it was becoming increasingly difficult to find stable ground, their feet being sucked into muddy patches and deep puddles.

Finally they made it to the riverbank. Although visibility was murky, Kirra could instantly tell that wading across the river was no longer an option. The deluge, as forceful as a bucket of water dumped on a flat rock, had already made the river swell with churning whitewater, and all manner of logs and driftwood were smashing against one another as they raced down the raging current.

"Oh no!" Luwan cried.

They could hear, even over the chaos of the boiling river, the Takers crashing and hacking through the brush behind them. Close.

Kirra scanned the riverbank. They could *not* be caught on this side with the Takers.

And that's when she got her idea. She pulled fiercely on Luwan's arm. "Follow me!"

They raced along the river's edge together. After a few moments, the Takers burst through the brush and screamed bloody oaths at them in that strange tongue.

Kirra did not even look back. She had eyes only for her destination.

When they reached the ferry post, Luwan shouted, "Do you know how to work the raft?"

"No time!" Kirra yelled back. She doubted the raft-pulley system would function under these conditions anyway. Instead, she leaped from the shore as far as she could and grabbed on to the rope with both hands. Her body swung forward, and she lunged with her legs to hook her ankles over the line.

Hanging upside down now, the raging river just a few feet below her head, she worked the rope hand over hand, sliding her feet down its length, and started to inch her way across the water to the other side. Luwan followed.

Their skill in tree-climbing helped tremendously, all those years of trusting grip and balance and lithe muscles to get them around. But their progress still seemed agonizingly slow, especially with the Takers racing along the shore at them, bellowing war cries.

"Kirra, look out!" Luwan screamed.

She turned her head and looked upriver. Rushing right toward them was an enormous log, the sharp ends of broken branches jutting out at odd angles along its length. It was going to smash right into them.

Kirra pulled with tired arms and legs, lifting her body and arching her back so that she was as flush with the rope as she could get. The log blasted by underneath with inches to spare. One of the jagged branch edges scraped a line of white-hot pain across her calf.

When it had passed, she tilted her head to look behind. Good news: Luwan had survived the rampaging log. Bad news: The Takers had reached the ferry post.

Kirra looked forward again and redoubled her efforts to pull herself across the line. She was roughly halfway across the river.

The rope sagged as a Taker jumped on the line and started to make his way toward them.

As the line drooped, Kirra sank dangerously close to the water. Another runaway log would kill her.

Something whistled past her ear. When it clattered among the river stones on the opposite shore, she realized it was an arrow.

She closed her eyes, knew she couldn't control any of that. Blocking out the bloodthirsty screams of the Takers and the roar of the whitewater frothing below her, she breathed in and out as she worked the rope: hand over hand, slide feet down, repeat.

Finally her feet knocked up against the ferry pole. She had made it.

Kirra dropped to the ground. Her arms and legs were shaky and weak from exertion, but she managed to reach up to help Luwan do the same. They were both shivering, soaked from the downpour as well as the spray of the raging river.

One of the Takers was still working his way across the rope, merely a few yards away. Four others had hopped onto the raft and were starting across, trying to keep their balance as the rough water rocked it back and forth. Only the leader stood on the opposite shore, that curious bow in his hands.

Kirra and Luwan clasped hands and turned to run for the forest. If they could just make it into the trees, they would have the advantage. No way would the Takers be able to find them among the branches.

But after only a few steps, Kirra's leg cramped and she tumbled to the ground, slamming her knee into a rock. Luwan pulled her to her feet but she was limping now, and even though he was strong enough to help drag her, they still had so much ground to cover.

She looked back at the raft. The Takers would be on the riverbank in just moments. She and Luwan weren't going to make it.

"AAARRRGGGHHH!"

Another war cry, but this one came from their side of the river.

Loba burst out from the forest, holding his largest cutting stone overhead with both hands, running full speed toward them, his long hair and beard streaming out behind him, mouth open in an enraged scream and eyes wild.

It was a terrifying sight, and the most beautiful thing that Kirra had ever seen.

He rushed right past them and brought the cutting stone down on the ferry post with a great clunk. The rope snapped in two cleanly, and the Taker who'd been shimmying across it was dumped into the roiling whitewater. Without the rope to anchor them, the men on the raft were swept away and out of sight in an instant.

The leader on the other side of the river looked downstream, stunned. The bow hung uselessly from his grip at his side.

Finally the Taker turned and regarded the trio at the opposite ferry post. He cupped his hands around his mouth and shouted over the roar of the river.

"I will return!" he bellowed. He took a deep breath and added, "WE will return!" Then he stalked across the riverbank and disappeared into the brush.

21

KIRRA AND LUWAN sat in front of the hut's cook fire, wrapped in blankets and holding warm cups of tea.

Maham brought them hot strips of meat. Kirra was so achy and tender that her body felt like one big bruise. But a full belly and the safety of home were helping her feel like herself again.

"Thank you so much," she said as Maham placed two more strips of meat on her plate.

"You're welcome, dear." Maham leaned in and whispered

to both of them, "I kept him at bay as long as I could. Said you needed to heal up and rest. But I'm afraid he will be back soon, with some serious questions."

Luwan nodded. "We know. It's okay. Thanks, Mother."

She gave them both a kiss on the forehead, tears in her eyes, then stood up as Loba entered the hut, all business. "We need to discuss this further."

Kirra and Luwan nodded. Loba knew the basics—they had shown him the giant puppet on the way home, while Teeha and the others had told him about the initial attack and Luwan's abduction. But Kirra knew he would want more.

Loba removed his cloak and hung it up. He sighed heavily and sat down in front of the kids.

He held their gaze for several unnerving minutes before finally speaking. "We will go over your punishments later. This meeting is to discuss what we are going to do now."

"Punishments?" Luwan said. His finger gingerly circled the burns on his chest, perhaps a visual reminder that he'd been punished plenty already.

Loba wasn't having it. "Going to the river. Going *across* the river. Sneaking off with your friends to work on secret projects. Bringing unwanted attention to our forest home. Attacking an armed group of men, unprovoked." He shook his head wearily. "Were you trying to break every rule you could possibly think of?"

"But, Father! I was only trying to help—"

"This is my fault, Loba," Kirra said. "The punishments should be entirely mine."

Loba shifted his hard stare toward her.

"But before that, I need you to listen to me," she said. "Really listen. We need to prepare for what's coming."

"Children do not tell their elders to listen." His voice had gone quiet and calm again, which Kirra found deeply unsettling. She was shaking inside but pressed on.

"I'm sorry, Loba. I mean no disrespect. But you heard what that hunter said before he left. He will be back. *They* will be back."

"It's the same thing he told me when I was captured," Luwan added. "He said they were going to bring more men back here."

"I can confirm that it's true," Kirra said quietly. She studied the floor.

Loba looked back and forth between the two of them before settling his gaze on Kirra. "And how do you know that?"

She took a deep breath. "Because . . ." Her voice faltered. It was one thing to remember, to admit it to herself. But it was quite another to say it out loud. Luwan slipped his hand into hers, gave it an encouraging squeeze. "Because these are the same people who took over my first home. Before I came here. I escaped, but they . . ." A tear spilled down her cheek. "No one else made it out."

Maham slipped over and put her arms around Kirra's shoulders. Luwan continued to squeeze her hand. Even Loba reached out and patted her affectionately.

They all sat that way for a while, holding Kirra and letting her cry it out before she was able to collect herself.

Finally, she shook her head and spoke again. "We can't let that happen to anyone here. We should leave immediately, and try to convince the rest of the Tree Folk to do the same. I know it won't be easy, but we can do our best."

"Leave?" Maham said.

"Where would we go?" Luwan asked.

Loba was studying Kirra. "Why have you not talked about these people before?"

"Hush, Loba," said Maham. "Can't you see the poor thing is—"

"It's okay," Kirra said. "It's a reasonable question." She took another deep breath. "I was trying desperately not to think about it. I blocked it out. Remembering my family . . . it was just too much."

"And we understand, dear." Maham squeezed her shoulders again.

Loba was still looking intently at her. "Can you tell us *why* they attacked your people? Anything that would help us make a plan moving forward?"

Kirra swallowed hard. She was absolutely certain that a full confession would be the best way to handle this moment . . . and yet she couldn't do it. Couldn't bear for this family to turn on her, be repulsed by her. So she shrugged and quietly said, "I don't know. They just showed up one day. Our people were caught unprepared. I was lucky to escape." She shivered all over. "I'm telling you, we should pack up and leave right now."

"I hear what you're saying, Kirra. But even if we decide to do that, we would not need to leave today. The rainy season will last for several months, and while it's here, no strangers will be crossing that river."

"I know. But as soon as the waters lower, they will come. And we will be helpless."

Luwan scoffed. "What's all this talk about running? Didn't you see them falling all over themselves to get away from our giant? What we need is an *army* of giants." He smacked his fist into the wooden floor. "We'd fight them so hard they would never return."

"You know that's impossible," Kirra said. "Please don't get me wrong—I am so grateful for what you and your friends did, but the only reason it worked is because you caught them by surprise. When they come back, they'll be ready. And they won't be afraid."

Loba shook his head. "She's right. Use your sense, boy. It took you and your friends over a week to build that thing.

And it didn't even have a body! You would need hundreds of people, all working from sunrise to sundown, to build enough of those things to stand up to a real army."

An image flashed in Kirra's mind. Peering under the rocks with Mome, seeing the bivouac ants and their structure made of thousands of bodies. Each small component of the community weak on its own but strong as a unit. All of them, working perfectly in unison to protect their most precious assets.

She looked around at each member of the family. "But . . . we *do* have hundreds of people. . . ."

Loba wrinkled his brow. "What do you mean?"

Kirra made a sweeping gesture with her arm, indicating the forest all around the hut. "The Tree Folk. This affects all of them. Instead of warning them and telling them to leave the forest—"

"We could ask them to help build an army of giants!" Luwan jumped in. "And we could make them even better! It was Teeha's idea to make the arm into a weapon, right? Well, she had lots of other amazing plans, but we just didn't have enough time to do all of them. She had even figured out a way to make them walk if we had enough people! We could be an unstoppable force. I bet we could—"

Loba held up his hand to cut Luwan off. "This is foolishness. There's no sense in even talking about it."

It was silent for a few moments before Kirra worked up the courage to say, "Why?"

Loba scowled. "What do you mean? Because Tree Folk families keep to themselves and always have, that's why. We take care of our own and do for the people we know. It is our way."

"But the Takers coming back will affect everyone!" Luwan said.

Maham cleared her throat. "The people in this forest have never been faced with a threat like this before," she said quietly. "They may have the capacity to change if the situation is dire enough."

Loba looked around the hut, saw that he was outnumbered. "I need to think about this." He stood and walked out the door.

Kirra, Luwan, and Maham sat silently. They had spoken together for an hour or so after Loba left, and made some plans of their own, but they had talked themselves out. None of it would happen if Loba disagreed.

It was well past dark when he came back. He stood by the cook fire, and the dying embers made shadows play across his face. They all looked up at him in anticipation, waited for him to speak first.

"So"—he looked at Kirra—"what is it, exactly, that you are proposing?"

Kirra stood and met his gaze. "If we can get all the Tree Folk in one place at the same time, I can speak to them. I will explain. I will make them understand what needs to be done, and ask for their help."

"And if they refuse? Which they will, I have no doubt."

"Then we leave the forest, protect this family. The others will have to make their own decisions."

Loba dropped his head and ran his fingers through his hair for several moments. At last he looked back up. "And how will we gather everyone?"

"My friends and I can do it!" Luwan said. "We'll start in the morning and go from tree to tree. Say there is an important gathering and the fate of the entire forest rests on the outcome."

"Not everyone will come," Maham said gently. "But I am willing to bet that enough show up to make a difference."

Loba considered the three expectant faces and sighed heavily. Then he stared directly at Kirra. "If we do this, it's going to be my name on the line. And if the meeting does not go well, I'm sure we will be strongly encouraged to leave this forest even if the Takers never come back."

Kirra stood up straight. "I will do my very best to convince them. I'll tell them my story."

He waited a long time to respond, so long that Kirra thought the entire plan might be scuttled. But finally he spoke. "This family has put its trust in you." Loba pointed a thick finger at Kirra. "Your story," he said, fixing her with his gaze, "had better be good."

Part Three
The Forest Giants

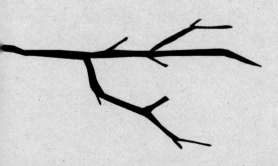

22

KIRRA SAT ATOP THE ROCKY RIDGE by the lake in the soft morning light, trying to calm her nerves. Besides Luwan, Loba, and Maham sitting beside her, the clearing was empty. They had been waiting for over half an hour, and she could tell from their uneasy silence that the others were feeling more than a little edgy, too.

As she looked around at the bare trees and vacant meadow, Kirra honestly didn't know which was more unsettling to think about—having to make a speech in front of the entire

Tree Folk community . . . or the prospect of no one showing up at all.

Finally, Loba spoke in a half whisper. "Are you sure you and your friends told everybody that the meeting was this morning?"

"Of course, Father!" Luwan shook his head. "I'm not a child anymore, you know."

"All will be well." Maham placed a hand on Kirra's and Luwan's shoulders. "This is just a very unusual request for these people. It may take them some extra time."

Several more minutes passed and still nobody came. For moral support, Kirra stole glances at the place where Mome had shown her the bivouac ants' remarkable structure. Stronger together. If only people would turn up, she would try to make them see that.

Luwan started to scowl and fidget with his hands, which didn't ease anyone's anxiety, but then she saw him break into a huge grin. Kirra looked questioningly at him and he pointed. She turned to see Teeha silently stepping into the clearing from behind a tree. The master builder was followed by six people who could only be her parents and brothers, as they all shared the same stoic expression. They were also all carrying large knapsacks. Teeha briefly lifted her hand in greeting, and her family wordlessly sat down in the wild grass.

Shortly after that, Makina emerged from the tree line on

the opposite side of the surrounding woods, leading a gaggle of younger sisters even tinier than her. She waved enthusiastically, and her sisters imitated her, all with beaming smiles. Kirra returned both the smile and the wave, which helped allay her nervousness a bit.

Finally, Kharee and Mozan entered. But they were by themselves. Could they not talk their parents into coming? If Luwan's friends couldn't even get their families here, what hope did they have for anyone else showing up? The butterflies started to flutter in Kirra's belly once again.

Well, at least a few Tree Folk were here. They would just have to . . .

It was hard to say when it started, because the people of the forest were so quiet and moved with such stealth, but as Kirra looked around at the surrounding trees, she realized that it was definitely more than a few.

People parted leaves in the upper branches to see out, revealing huddled groups of three or four sharing a wide branch. Others dropped from low-hanging limbs to sit at the base of a trunk, while some were bold enough to step out of the forest and sit in the open. And some had perhaps been there all along, seated among the branches, their camouflage clothing and natural stillness allowing them to blend in with the woods.

Over the next several minutes, the forest surrounding the clearing filled with people. Kirra turned her neck as far as it could go in both directions and took them all in. There must have been several hundred gathered here. And they kept coming. Perhaps over a thousand? Even two thousand? Kirra would never have dreamed there were this many Tree Folk.

And had she really thought she was nervous before? That was just a mild case of the jitters. Now it felt like she couldn't breathe. Though none of these people knew it, their fate rested on Kirra's words and how much she could encourage and inspire them to respond. It all depended on her.

When the emergence of newcomers slowed to a trickle and finally appeared to stop, Loba stood up on top of the ridge and surveyed all the eyes looking down at him from the surrounding trees. Kirra noticed his hands were trembling before he clasped them together and took a deep breath.

"My name is Loba. I was born in the branches, as was my father and his father before him." He was speaking loudly but not shouting. There was no need. The people in the clearing were so quiet and focused that his voice was able to carry to the entire assembly.

"I am not a man of many words, but my family and I want to thank you for coming here this morning. We know this is unusual. After spending my entire life in this forest, I do not remember a single time that all of us were called together. It is not in our nature to decide things as a group. We take care of our own and let others do as they will."

Loba swallowed heavily, appearing to search for the right

thing to say. This clearly did not come naturally to him, and Kirra's heart swelled with gratitude knowing that he was going through with it solely on the basis of her word.

"Anyway . . . I say this because you must know I do not treat this lightly. But events have taken place recently that could have dire consequences for all of us. And we will be asking for your help to put things back in order so you may all go on living your lives as normal."

Loba turned and motioned to Kirra, who stood up. She felt very small in the middle of all those people. "This is Kirra. She was not born in the branches. She did not start out this life as one of us." Loba turned and looked right into her eyes as he spoke. "But I have come to trust her. And respect her. I never thought I would say this about an out-sider before I met her, but we have fully accepted Kirra into our family. I consider her my daughter. And if you have any trust for me as a lifelong member of the Tree Folk, I would like you to extend the same respect to her as she speaks with you now."

Kirra, standing there before the entire crowd, didn't know whether to thank Loba or curse him. His public sup-port certainly helped steady her nerves . . . but how was she supposed to speak around the lump that was forming in her throat? It had been so long since someone had called her *daughter*, and she'd thought she would never hear that word again.

Brushing a stray tear from the corner of one eye, she took a shaky but deep breath and spun around slowly to take in her audience. And as she did so, a warm and familiar feeling of calm washed over her as she realized something very important.

This was a storytellers' circle.

She could see that now. And how many times had she watched the first man who called her daughter perform in front of an audience? Perhaps not a crowd this big, of course, but was there really any difference? She had seen Taro speak to groups of the elderly, or hordes of children, gatherings of families, and unfamiliar faces in distant villages. She had observed him closely, studied the ways he drew people in and delivered the goods. She had also kept an eye on the crowds and discovered something else: Everyone loved a good story. Taro was skilled, for certain, but at the end of the day, he was merely giving the people what they wanted.

And her father—her first father—had chosen her Helper position perfectly. Taro had seen it before she had: This was what Kirra had been born to do.

If Taro had felt she was capable of carrying on his legacy and telling meaningful stories that made an impact on others . . . If Loba trusted her, and so did Maham and Luwan and his friends . . . then she knew she could do this. The nerves melted away and she began to speak.

"As Loba says, I was not born here. But the place where

I come from had many similarities. We also hid ourselves from the outside world. My ancestors built a perfect community deep inside the hollow crater of a dormant volcano."

Kirra described the towering walls of stone that protected Zedu like a fortress, throwing her hands in the air to illustrate their formidable vastness. She paced around the ridge in a circle, describing the various clans on the different terraces that lined the interior, and how they worked together to bring resources to all the people in the community. Making broad gestures to the surrounding trees and meadow and lake, she praised the natural beauty of the land of the Tree Folk and explained that the Zeduans also had a respect for nature and similarly sought to live in harmony with their surroundings.

Her voice grew stronger as she described her native home. It was the opposite of a Memory Trap; instead of letting the dark things in her past drag her down, the bright and beautiful things she had experienced were infusing her with confidence and power. To remember everything—both the good and the bad—was to honor those whom she had loved.

She rotated, taking in her entire audience. "When you have been born and raised in such a special place, and taught to respect your lands and live within their means—as all of you have been lucky enough to experience—it can be difficult to understand those who do not. It can, in fact, be difficult to even acknowledge that such people could exist."

She paused dramatically, because she knew it was something Taro would have done at that point. That was another memory that lifted her up and empowered her once she allowed it to come back.

During the pause, she scanned the crowd, establishing direct eye contact with as many people as she could, forging a personal connection with her audience, just like she had been taught. Finally, she spoke again.

"But I have met such people."

Then she slipped from Storyteller into Actor, as all good tale spinners must do at times. As she described Red Streak addressing his troops, she became the man. She puffed up her chest and made her voice gruff, using hand gestures to suggest his bulging muscles, intimidating armor, and cruel weaponry. She imitated him as he bullied the Nafaluu captive and snarled bloody orders at his men.

With a rush of pride, she noticed something happening in the crowd—the same thing she had observed when her first father competed in the storytelling competitions. People were turning to one another, nodding in approval or making faces to their neighbor that said *Oh, my, did you hear that?* She knew they were with her. Time to press on.

"And now these people have come to our lands. You may have noticed them in the last few weeks, crossing the river at its lowest point and hunting in our forests. And if you saw them, then you must have noticed that each one carried as much game as possible, trip after trip after trip. It's not hunting; it's plunder. That is their nature. My people called them the Takers because that's what they do—they take beyond reason."

She swept her hands with a flourish to indicate the surrounding woods. "You have all learned the lesson, passed down from each generation, to leave a healthy population of each type of beast so the hunt may continue the next season. Why, even the Hook Hunters have enough sense to follow that rule." This earned a ripple of laughter through her audience.

Now that she had them, really had them, it was time to lower the hammer. Get to the meat of this meeting. "But these Takers cannot be reasoned with. And they have discovered our little corner of paradise in this world.

"They have warned us." She paced a bit. "No, that's not quite right." Another pause, another scanning of the crowd. "They have *threatened* us. They have vowed to return after the rainy season ends and the river becomes crossable again. The best outcome we can hope for is that they wipe out the entire store of beasts, fish, and birds in the forest, and make our home unlivable.

"The more likely scenario, however, is that they not only do that, but also destroy the trees and enslave us. Or worse. Simply wipe us out."

Kirra paused and took a deep breath, but not for dramatic

effect. Because she knew this next part would be difficult to say. She didn't dress it up with any storytelling tricks or flourishes. She just said, simply, "That's what happened to my beloved community. The Takers barged in, took what they wanted, and burned the rest. I am the only survivor of my people."

Kirra found strength in the fact that she had gotten through that part without breaking down in tears. Her voice was clear and powerful when she said, "They must be stopped when they return. And we are the only ones who can stop them."

It was silent for a good long spell while this information sank into the crowd. Until an older man, his customary beard long and gray, stood up from where he had been sitting at the base of a nearby tree. "I'd like to ask a question."

Kirra turned to face him. "Yes?"

"Well, these Taker people found us because the river got lower than normal with the long dry season. So they came over here to hunt." The man pulled on his beard, glancing around at the crowd and seeming to realize for the first time just how many people he was addressing. But he gathered his courage and pressed on. "You never told us how it happened at the volcano place, though. I mean, if you were all so well hidden for so long . . . how did they find you?"

Kirra calmly looked back at the man. Instead of being filled with dread at this question, as she expected would happen, she felt a sense of relief. If she were ever truly going to be a part of the Tree Folk, a full member of Luwan's family, she was going to have to be honest. About everything. And if they kicked her out, then that was what was meant to be. She would prefer an honest exile to staying here in deceit.

She pivoted to look at Luwan's family, making eye contact with each of them in turn, and then faced the old man again. "It was my fault," she said loudly. "I snuck out one night against the will of my parents. I wanted to gather information on the Takers—to help protect my community. I found their camp, but I became frightened of what I discovered. I lost my nerve and escaped, and I tried to sneak back home, but they followed me. It all happened very quickly after that. Over the course of the next day and night, my community was destroyed."

Kirra hadn't truly noticed the pressing weight that had been stooping her shoulders and bearing down on her chest for years, making it difficult for her to take a full breath, until it lifted with those words.

She felt new. Remade.

It was completely quiet in the clearing after Kirra's confession. She stood there, very still, and waited for whatever would come next.

"Loba!" someone called from high up in a tree. "Why did you bring her into our forest? She admits to already destroying one community."

"Yeah!" A cry from the other side of the clearing. "She's dangerous. Why should we listen to her?"

"She doesn't belong here!"

"She never belonged here!"

There were rumblings from all sides. Loba shifted uneasily, looking unsure how to respond.

Kirra had the same thought she'd had in the hunters' camp: People were capable of anything when they were scared.

One man broke away from those sitting in the clearing, standing up and stalking directly toward the ridge. Kirra tensed.

But as he got closer, Kirra recognized the braids and the smooth, easy gait. She started to breathe again.

Mome climbed up the side of the ridge, his scarred and powerful hands finding sure grip on the stone. He stood beside Kirra and stared down the audience until the murmured protests faded completely. Then he addressed the assembly.

"I, too, was not born in the branches. I have traveled widely across this big world." He pointed around at the crowd. "This has been a reason many of you don't trust me fully. I accept that. However, it is the main reason you should listen to me now and heed my words.

"You people are fortunate to have spent all your days here.

This is a special place. It is beautiful and peaceful, and you have taken good care of it.

"But while what you have here is unique, there are, unfortunately, people like the Takers all over, in every land." He put his arm around Kirra. "This brave young lady did not bring the Takers to her home. They were already on their way. They started their inevitable march to that volcano when time began.

"Yes, perhaps the actions of a frightened young girl cracked the door open a bit sooner than it might have been opened otherwise. But the Takers were coming, and they would have kicked down that door eventually no matter what."

He paused, looking around slowly, eyes boring into any member of the audience who dared to meet his gaze. "And now they are on *your* doorstep. How you choose to deal with them is up to you."

Mome raised his voice, and it rang out to every corner of the clearing. "This girl is not condemning you. She is trying to save you. And you would do well to respect her words and do what she says."

He pulled Kirra closer and hugged her. "Did you hear what I said, meerkat?" he whispered in her ear. "The terrible things that happened were not your fault. You have to understand that."

She had been waiting years for someone to say these words. Mome had not just said them to her; he had stood there in the first public meeting in Tree Folk history and told everyone. She had no words of her own beyond *thank you*.

She felt more arms around her and looked up to see that Maham had joined them. She was quickly followed by Luwan and Loba. All four of them held a grateful Kirra in their collective embrace.

Teeha left her brothers and climbed the ridge, then Makina and Kharee and Mozan did the same.

The little group huddled together on the outcropping of stone, loving and supporting Kirra in front of everyone who made up their world.

Finally, the man with the gray beard spoke up again, loud enough for everyone in the clearing to hear. "I heard your story, young woman. With my ears"—he thumped his chest—"and with my heart." He pulled on his beard and looked around at the audience before turning back to Kirra. "Okay, then. What is it you want us to do?"

23

TEEHA MOTIONED TO HER BROTHERS, and they made their way to the top of the ridge carrying large knapsacks. They pulled pieces of wood and lengths of rope out of the pouches, knelt on the stone, and began assembling something. The crowd didn't move, hardly seemed to breathe, just watched silently. Kirra couldn't help but grin as she realized that if this were the first-ever story time for the Tree Folk, they were definitely getting a show worthy of the occasion.

When the boys stood up, they were holding three human-size puppets with fearsome visages carved into the wood. There were joints built in, the separate pieces of wood tethered by rope, which allowed the puppets free range of motion.

Kirra gave Teeha a questioning look, nodded to the puppets, and then gestured to the crowd. "Would you like to explain how they work to everyone?" she whispered.

Teeha was mortified. Eyes wide and making an expression that looked like she'd smelled something bad, she shook her head fiercely and immediately sat down.

"I think that might be a *no*," Luwan whispered to Kirra.

"Okay, I'll take it from here." She smiled at both of them, then turned to address the crowd again.

"These Takers are bigger than us. Stronger," Kirra said in a loud voice. "They have cruel weapons and protective clothing.

"But"—she held up a finger—"we have some advantages on our side. The first and most important is that, if we have to fight, we'll be fighting in these woods. Every single one of you knows this terrain by heart, and how to travel swiftly and quietly through the trees."

Kirra spread her arms to indicate everyone gathered in the clearing. "That's why it's so good to see all of you here today. Individually, your familiarity with the forest is incredible. But together, combining all that knowledge as one cohesive unit? We will be able to do anything."

She walked over to where Teeha's brothers were still

holding the puppets. "And that brings me to the last part of our strength. The plan we want to share with you today.

"Good ideas can come from anywhere. One of the smallest among us came up with the idea that's going to defeat the Takers." Kirra motioned to Makina, who crossed the ridge to stand beside her. Kirra put her arm around her friend and said, "It was Makina here who, after seeing the Takers, said, 'I wish we could be giants, just like them.'"

Titters of laughter were heard around the circle.

"Yes, it's an idea that some would laugh at," Kirra acknowledged. "But luckily it fell on creative ears. And now it's the idea that will save us."

Makina grinned widely and waved at the crowd. Her pack of tiny sisters clapped enthusiastically and waved right back, to the delight of the audience.

"Our friend Teeha is an amazing builder," Kirra continued. "Give her some raw materials and a little bit of inspiration, and she can create anything. So, after she heard Makina's idea, she decided to make a giant of her own."

Kirra went back into Storyteller mode then. Using the puppets on the ridge as models, she described in vivid detail the twenty-foot forest giant that Teeha had constructed, and how her friends had worked the levers and pulleys to make it shout and stomp and throw great rocks.

She explained how, if everyone here worked together under Teeha's direction, they could form an army of their own. If some people were willing to help make the figures, there could be many more giants. Then others could learn how to operate them. Again using the puppets, she showed where the Tree Folk would be situated within each giant to make it move. The first time, the kids had had only one week to prepare. Now they had several months of rainy season to use before the river receded and the Takers came back.

"When I was still with my first community, back in the volcano, my mother and father had different ideas about how to deal with these Takers. My mother wanted to fight to defend our home. But my father wanted to protect the community peacefully, with his stories."

Kirra paused for a few moments. After years of trying to forget Maja and Paja, who'd been everything to her, it felt so good—so right—to honor their memory now by speaking publicly about them.

"But we will use *both* approaches when we defend ourselves. We will fight, but with a kind of story—a visual one. A symbol of our strength.

"And speaking of stories, if we're successful, the Takers will spread ours for us. They will tell all their people, far and wide, about the great and terrible forest giants that fought to protect this land. Most communities have to keep fighting, generation after generation, but these tales will fight our future battles for us. We will only need to do this once, and the stories will protect our people for generations to come."

Kirra ended with a final description of how the first giant battle had ended, the Takers falling all over themselves as they scurried back to the other side of the river and away from the giant as fast as they possibly could.

When she finished, the crowd erupted into cheers. Luwan and his friends waved to the audience from their spot atop the rocky ridge, basking in the adoration.

Mome stood by Kirra again after the applause died down. "We thank you for listening to all of us this morning," he said. "It is, however, very important to face the truth if you decide to join us in defending our woods. It will be difficult. There will be losses. So please listen now. Anyone who wants to leave the forest and move elsewhere, you are free to do so. We will not stop you nor say an ill word about you. Furthermore, anyone who wants to stay but would prefer not to get involved, we understand. No one will be forced into this.

"But we do believe this is our only chance, the one way to save everything we hold dear."

Loba also stood up again to speak. "So we are officially asking now for your help. If a handful of children can fight off a half-dozen warriors, just imagine what an entire united community could do against them."

He raised a hand in the air and kept it there as he slowly turned in a circle to address the entire crowd. "Members of the Tree Folk, you who are branch-born . . . who will stand with us?"

The old man with the gray beard was the first to raise his hand. Others followed right away. After a few moments, Kirra scanned the entire crowd but could not find a single person without their hand up.

Even though the Takers didn't know it yet, the next battle had already begun.

24

THE NEXT FEW MONTHS were a whirlwind of activity. Where once the forest had seemed eerily deserted, now it was teeming with people. Everyone was out of their homes, even in the pouring rain, no longer feeling uncomfortable about being in the open.

It was a prolonged period of trial followed by a whole lot of error. For every step the community took forward, it seemed like they took two lurching, shambling steps backward. Literally. Because making the giants mobile turned out to be a lot more difficult than it seemed. Teeha could rig up the logs to make them stomp in place, as their first giant had done when it scared that small group of hunters. But making those stomps cross some distance was a different story altogether.

On one soggy afternoon, Kirra sat on a great stump with Teeha, Luwan, and Makina, watching two different groups of builders test out their designs.

Makina pointed. "They look so weird without the rest of the bodies."

Kirra nodded. The girl had a point. The twelve-foot-high wooden legs ended suddenly at the waist in midair. It was a little creepy.

"Group One, take your places." Teeha's voice, timid in conversation, was strong and clear when she was giving directions.

Six Tree Folk, four men and two women, scaled the logs that made up the legs, hands grabbing levers and feet positioned on pedals.

"Ready?" Teeha called.

The woman at the top of the contraption was quick to give a thumbs-up.

"Go!"

The legs took three tiny stuttering steps followed by one long lunge; then they twisted in a patch of mud and promptly toppled over. The Tree Folk all jumped out, keeping clear of the falling logs but landing squarely in the muck.

"Everyone okay?" Kirra yelled. The Tree Folk picked themselves off the ground, filthy and sheepish but unhurt.

"That looked like my little sister trying to walk," Makina whispered. "She's one and a half years old."

Luwan giggled, and Kirra slapped at him to keep him quiet.

"Ready, Group Two?"

Another thumbs-up, but this one perhaps a bit less enthusiastic.

"Go!"

One leg stayed firmly planted in place while the other stepped frantically, winding in a furious circle. Eventually both tilted and crashed to the ground, where the one mobile leg kept kicking in the air.

"That looks like my dad . . . after he's had too many cups of strong mead," Luwan said.

Now it was Makina's turn to giggle. Kirra slapped at them both, but they quickly stopped when they saw Teeha's reaction.

The girl moaned, cradling her head in both hands while she stared down at the fallen legs. "I've tried everything," she muttered, shaking her head back and forth in frustration. "I don't know how to fix it."

She was clearly talking to herself, but Kirra put a soothing hand on her shoulder and responded. "You'll get it. We still have more time." Kirra said this as much to calm her own nerves as to comfort her friend. Each rainy day was a blessing for them, but she knew the wet season would not last forever.

"Excuse me?" Teeha and Kirra looked up to see a young man approaching the stump. "I . . . well, you know more about this than me, of course . . . but I might be able to help? I mean maybe with just this one thing?"

Teeha lifted her head out of her hands and studied him. "How so?"

He turned and waved for them to follow. "It will be easier if I show you."

His name was Subon, and his home tree was quite a distance away. When they got close, he stepped off a trail and pushed aside a group of hanging creepers that had been concealing the ladder to his front door.

"This feels so different." Subon held the vines aside and motioned for them to climb the ladder. "We usually do everything we can to hide our place. I'm not used to showing people right where it is."

"Maybe things are changing." Kirra gave him a smile. "Could be a whole new day for the Tree Folk."

Subon smiled back, and Kirra felt shy all of a sudden. "Well, maybe I don't mind those changes," he said.

Teeha rolled her eyes. "Hurry up and show us why you brought us here." As usual, she was all business.

They climbed up to the porch that wrapped around his

house. "So I have a little sister, okay? And she's always waking me up in the middle of the night to get her some water. And if our gourd is empty, I have to climb all the way down to the pond and fill up a cup for her. By the time I get back, I'm so wide-awake I can't get back to sleep."

"Aw, that's so sweet of you!" Kirra said.

Teeha grunted. "Get on with the story."

Subon reached through an open window and brought out an upside-down wooden cup with rope tied around it. "So I rigged this up." He pulled on the rope in a hand-over-hand gesture. The rope was connected to round wooden pulleys that were fastened to the tree trunk at different points. As Subon tugged on the rope, Teeha and Kirra watched the cup travel down to the ground, dip into the spring, and flip right-side up. Then he hauled it right back up to where they were standing.

Subon grabbed the cup and took a long drink. "See? It's easy! She can do it by herself, and I get to stay asleep."

Teeha studied the system of pulleys carefully, not saying anything.

"Wow," Kirra said, smiling at Subon again. "Thanks so much for showing us this. It's a really clever way to—"

"Let's go." Teeha grabbed Kirra by the elbow and pulled her roughly to the ladder.

Subon stuck his face over the edge of the platform as they

descended. "Maybe you could come back sometime?" The look on his face was so hopeful.

"Oh, sure," Teeha said. "Right after the looming life-or-death battle."

Kirra shrugged and gave him a wave.

Two days later, Teeha had rigged up a system that connected ankle, knee, and waist with round pulleys and the giant puppets were walking smoothly.

And then she was on to the next challenge. Much to her chagrin, Teeha had become the most popular person in the community. People sought her out at all times of the day, asking for guidance about engineering and construction, but also bringing ideas and gadgets from their own homes, as Subon had done. It turned out the Tree Folk had a lot of good ideas when they were able to pool them together like this. Kirra was proud of the way her friend handled the attention. Teeha was very professional—not exactly warm—but she always studied each new design carefully and patiently answered each question and took the time to demonstrate this or that bit of mechanics with the smaller-scale puppets her brothers had made. In fact, she taught some people so well that they were able to go back and lead the building process in their section of the woods.

One morning, during a rare stretch of time when Teeha wasn't being bothered with requests, she approached Kirra at the edge of the forest, where Luwan had set up their base of operations. She had brought one of the smaller puppets along.

"Can I show you something?" Teeha asked.

"Of course." Kirra pushed herself off the ground and dusted herself off. "What is it?"

"Do you remember when Mozan said that 'the trees are the real giants'? Back when we were showing the first one to you?"

Kirra nodded.

"Well, that got me to thinking about something." She propped the puppet against a nearby trunk. "When we built the first giant, I designed it to be operated by just five people. Because it was only going to be our little group that was using it.

"But now? There are so many volunteers, we can have more people in each one. I bet we could put a dozen people into each giant puppet and still be able to make our army."

Kirra tilted her head and studied the puppet. "So does that mean you want to make them bigger?"

"Yes, we could do that." Teeha nodded. "But it also means we can make them do more. And the design could be different. Better. Here, I'll show you."

She started to disassemble the puppet. "With the first

giant, there were only a few moving parts. Because five of us had to move everything, right?" She lifted up various pieces she had just unattached. "But if we have more people operating each one, then we can have smaller moving parts, with each person responsible for their own segment."

Kirra wished that her mind worked more like Teeha's, but it just didn't. "I hear what you're saying, but I don't know how that helps us."

"Here, let me try to demonstrate," Teeha said. Kirra was grateful for her patience.

Teeha moved over to a sapling. "Okay, pretend this is a big tree." She took all the little pieces of the puppet and placed them in and around the tree. Some she rested on top of branches, running parallel so they ended up just looking like a thicker limb. Others she wedged in the crook of two branches, hidden behind a screen of leaves. And others she laid on the ground out at the base of the trunk, as if they were dead branches or fallen logs.

She stepped back to look over what she had just done and raised her eyebrows in a question at Kirra. "Does that look like a giant to you?"

Kirra shook her head. "Of course not. It just looks like a tree."

"Exactly. But if there is someone in charge of each piece, hiding in the branches, and they had all practiced to coordinate their movements with the whole group"—Teeha grabbed the individual pieces and quickly reassembled them into a puppet—"all of a sudden there is a giant there."

Kirra finally got it. "And that way we could hide our numbers!"

"Exactly." Teeha gave her a rare smile. "The Takers would enter what they think is an empty forest, and suddenly they'd be surrounded by giants."

"You are amazing." Kirra slowly shook her head in wonder. "Simply amazing. I'm so glad you're on our side."

Teeha ducked her head and picked up the puppet. Even with all the positive attention, she still hadn't gotten used to taking compliments. "I should get back to Luwan and the others. I want to test this out." She scurried away and disappeared into the forest.

Kirra stretched and sat down on the grass of the meadow. She deserved a five-minute break. She had worked harder these last several weeks than she ever had in her life.

As she was sitting there, a woman and several children walked by. They were carrying pots of food that smelled delicious and baskets full of bread. The little group stopped in front of Kirra.

"Would you like something to eat?"

Kirra leaned forward and peered into the pot. Freshly grilled crocodile steaks.

"Mmm. Yes, I would love some."

The woman smiled and fished out three strips of meat,

while one of her daughters broke off a hunk of bread. It was still warm from the oven.

"Oh, by the gods, this is the best thing I've eaten in a long time." This was no false praise. Not only was the meat skillfully prepared, but Kirra's entire family had been so busy each day that they hardly had time to wolf down leftovers at night before they fell into their hammocks.

"Thank you very much. It's my pleasure to be able to serve you."

Kirra wrinkled her brow. "Did someone ask you to do this? The person in charge of your construction group, perhaps?"

The woman motioned to her children to walk on without her for a moment. When they left, she turned back to Kirra and shook her head.

"No, nothing like that. I just . . . I'm afraid I'm no good at building, and besides, I need to look after my little ones during the day. But I still wanted to help, you know? I wanted to do my part."

"That's wonderful. Thank you so much."

"When I saw you speak in the clearing that day, I knew we would be staying to protect the forest. Like I said, I have no business building or fighting, but I know I can cook."

"You certainly can!"

"Anyway, I should be going. There are so many people to feed."

"Thanks again."

Kirra watched as the woman went from group to group throughout the clearing, the people at each workstation delighted to take a break from their arduous labor and get an unexpected treat in the bargain.

Over the next several weeks, Kirra regularly saw this woman bringing food to people throughout the clearing, and her example inspired others. Wherever Kirra roamed through the forest, checking on construction sites and trying to encourage the workers, she saw more and more people serving food to their fellow Tree Folk. And she heard the appreciative comments ring out:

"How did you get the meat so juicy?"

"What type of seasoning did you use?"

"Do you think I could stop by your hut sometime and you could show me how you've set up your cook fire? My meals never turn out like this."

One day as she sat in the clearing, enjoying a kebab of freshly grilled boar and mushrooms that had been given to her by a man wandering around with a cart full of them, Kirra realized that this was much bigger than food. These people were meeting others whom they never would have approached before. They were sharing, connecting.

She almost felt like she was back in Zedu again.

After nearly four months of nonstop toil, Kirra noticed that the rainstorms had started to abate. The river was still raging, but the dry season was at hand.

She was lying out on the platform surrounding the hut, her muscles tired and sore, when Luwan climbed onto the wooden boards and collapsed beside her.

They were quiet for a few moments before he said, "It feels different, doesn't it?"

She tilted her head and studied him. "What does?"

Luwan reached up and motioned to the surrounding forest. "Things are drying out. Rainy season will be over soon."

She nodded. "Yes . . ."

"Well, that's usually such a happy time, right? Hopeful. Everybody's dreaming about warm weather, and not having to wring out soggy clothes when you get home every night, and not having to slog through the mud to get anywhere. It's always the best part of the year."

Kirra nodded and sighed. "But not this time. This time it's all mixed up with—"

"Dread." Luwan rubbed his stomach. "It's like a cold ball sitting right here. Won't ever really go away."

Kirra thought about that. She had been living with her own dread for so long—trying to keep all those memories pushed away—that she supposed she hadn't noticed it as much as the others. Now that she had finally let go and told the truth, to herself and everyone else, she was feeling much better. Relieved. Even with the upcoming battle looming before her.

After that, Luwan was quiet for so long that she thought he had fallen asleep. Kirra couldn't blame him. He'd been working harder than anybody on their puppet, and at the end of each day he would go off by himself and come home late. She was usually asleep when he got back to the hut, or simply too tired to remember to ask him where he had been. Probably helping other construction groups, teaching them how to work together to maneuver the giants.

Finally he turned to her and whispered, "You know what I keep thinking?"

"What?"

"It's a good thing I pulled you out of the river that day a long time ago."

Kirra got up on her elbows. The memory of that time was still painful, and it didn't help that Luwan still thought about it, too. Would she ever be more than a pathetic orphan in his eyes?

"I'm very grateful to you, Luwan. You know that."

He waved her words away. "If I hadn't, none of this would be happening. We wouldn't all be working together. We wouldn't stand a chance against these intruders."

Kirra searched his face for any hint of sarcasm or teasing,

but he looked deadly serious. "I don't know about that," she said. "The Tree Folk still have you and your friends. Like Teeha, she is *amazing*. The other day, she——"

"I'm not talking about Teeha," he said. "I'm talking about *you*. You're amazing, too, Kirra. You have so much strength. . . ."

Her face flushed, and she almost laughed. He'd seen her at her absolute weakest moments. "Thanks, Luwan. I do think it's been good for me to remember and talk about . . . before."

"You're an incredibly brave person," he said. "That day you ran into the Takers' camp to rescue me, and that time you spoke in front of everyone . . . I couldn't have done those things."

Kirra was taken aback. He was the bravest person she knew. Foolhardy sometimes, yes, but still . . . She recovered quickly. "That's not true! You've never been one to shy away from danger."

He smiled at that.

"And it takes a lot of courage to be a good Hook Hunter," she went on. "Like you're going to be." She poked him in the ribs, and he squirmed out of reach, laughing.

They lay still for a few minutes after that, until Luwan said, "Can I ask you a question?"

"Of course."

"Do you think we're ready? I mean, really ready?"

Kirra took some time to ponder her answer, the way Mome always did for her. It was an important question and deserved a thoughtful response.

"Honestly? I don't think we'll know until it happens. How can you really prepare for something like this? We don't know how many of them will show up, and we don't know how the Tree Folk will respond in the moment." Kirra shuddered as she recalled her terrifying experiences in the two Taker camps. Luwan had called her brave, but she definitely hadn't felt that way either time. It was so easy to give in to panic and so difficult to keep your mind and body focused while everything was crashing down around you. "Practice is one thing, but being in the middle of a dangerous situation is another."

"That's not very comforting," Luwan said. "But it's fair."

She reached over and took his hand, squeezing it. "Whatever happens, I'm glad I'm doing this with you, your family, and your friends. Thank you for everything you've done for me."

"You got it, sis. We're in this together." He squeezed her hand back. "And whatever happens? I don't think we're going to have to wait much longer to find out."

25

A FEW DAYS LATER, Kirra was dozing in her hammock, when the blast of a great horn tore apart the silence of the jungle.

Her eyes flew open. The gravity of the situation hit her in an instant. This was really going to happen. Not another rehearsal with the giant puppets, and no more facing her enemy in a half-forgotten dream. She was going to actually see Takers again. Today.

It became very difficult to breathe.

Luwan's head popped down through the trapdoor.

"They're coming," he said.

She nodded, staring back at him, unblinking. Luwan tilted his head and studied her expression. "Are you going to be okay?"

Kirra forced herself to nod. "I can do this." It came out in a choked whisper.

"No." Luwan reached down for her. "*We* can do this."

She grabbed on to his hand, warm and strong just like all those years ago. The dread and panic abated a bit, replaced by something close to relief. Because she had been waiting for this moment ever since she had spoken in the clearing, and every day had been long hours spent in preparation.

No, that wasn't true, she realized. . . . She had actually been waiting for this day—whether she knew it or not—ever since she had been a terrified and devastated ten-year-old girl watching Zedu burn.

Today was the day she simply must do what had to be done.

When Kirra entered the hut, Loba and Maham were putting on hunting cloaks, which would camouflage them during what was to come. Loba was grim-faced in his preparation, slowly and deliberately lacing his boots, cinching his belt, and securing a cutting stone at his waist. He paused to give Kirra a quick nod in greeting, then got back about his business.

Maham was gathering her supplies, too. She and Loba would be part of a team operating one of the puppets that would be leading the ambush, so she needed to be in place right away. But when she saw Kirra, she ran over and gave her a fierce hug. Maham grabbed Luwan by the shoulder and pulled him in as well.

She wiped a tear from her eye and said, "You two be careful."

"Mother," Luwan said, "there's no being careful in a battle."

"Oh, I know. Just let me be a mother for a minute." Tears leaked from the corners of her eyes. "I'm so sorry." She wiped at her face. "I know we're doing the right thing, the only thing. Really. It's just . . . I love you both so much."

It was the first time Maham had ever said those words to her. She wanted to savor them, but that would have to wait. "We love you, too," Kirra said. She looked directly into the woman's eyes and took her by the shoulders. "And this evening, after we have protected the forest, we'll all meet back here and have dinner, okay? Together. As a family."

"That's a fine plan." Loba walked over to them. "I'll roast a haunch of boar. We can all have that to look forward to, yes?"

Kirra looked from face to face, trying desperately to keep the uncertainty she felt out of her eyes. The thought that all four of them might not make it back to this cozy hut was too much to bear, but dwelling on it would simply make it even more difficult to leave. So she waved good-bye, grabbed

Luwan's hand to pull him out the front door, and started to head in the direction of the river.

The woods were as busy as a wasps' nest as the pair made their way through the branches. People were bustling all around them, hauling sections of wood and lengths of rope, racing to the spot on the river where the Takers had first crossed over months ago, or setting up battle stations deeper in the forest. The Tree Folk were mostly silent as they went about their tasks, giving their fellow forest dwellers a quick nod of recognition as they passed.

Near the river, Kirra and Luwan reached the tree that had been designated their group's base of operations. Kharee and Mozan were already there, standing near the trunk, and Makina joined them shortly thereafter. Last was Teeha, marching in with her brothers, who would round out the contingent of fighters controlling their giant.

She walked up to them. "Should we try to gather everyone in this area quickly? Go over the plan once more?"

Luwan shook his head. "There's no time. Also, everyone knows the plan forward and backward. We've been over it a million times."

"I agree," Kirra said. "Just let everyone get ready in their own way."

Teeha nodded. "That works. Let's take our stations and get a look at what's headed this direction."

Makina was the first to scramble up the trunk and shoot into the branches. "Those stupid Takers are going to be sorry they ever woke up this morning!"

Mozan looked at the others and nodded appreciatively. "As far as battle cries go, that one's not bad."

"Enough talk." Kharee picked up his little brother and thrust him up into the lower limbs of the tree. "Let's go."

Kirra followed, climbing halfway up the trunk to find her section of the giant puppet. They had stored it there a few weeks earlier and had worked with it dozens of times since. She ran her hands across the wood. They had practiced with it so much that she found touching its grainy surface comforting.

That feeling of comfort dissipated, however, when she brushed aside a screen of leaves and got her first look at the river.

There were hundreds of Takers on the other side.

She felt the same disbelief as when the entire Tree Folk community had assembled to listen to her months ago. How could there even be so many of them?

Soldiers filled the riverbank, standing shoulder to shoulder

in perfectly straight lines, those long gray faces staring sto-
ically across the water. As others poured out of the scrub
brush and joined the ranks, there was no hurrying or
rushing about. Their movements were precise, measured,
methodical. That was more unnerving than a screaming,
frenzied charge would have been. A cold pit formed deep in
her stomach when Kirra realized that the people of the forest weren't the only ones who had spent months training for
this moment.

In fact, it looked like the Takers had spent years practicing for battle. For these soldiers spread out in front of them,
it might have been their entire lives.

And Kirra noticed that they had tailored their appearance for just such a battle as this one. The first time she had
encountered the Takers, they had looked completely out of
place in the environment, their leathery skin and war attire
looking much more suited to a desert landscape. But not this
time. They had dyed their leather and armor a dull green
and brown to match the camouflage of the Tree Folk, even
going so far as to adorn their clothing with leaves and bits of
branches. Kirra swallowed heavily. They had obviously put a
lot of thought and preparation into coming here and wiping
out her people.

The warriors in the first several rows carried long spears or
oversize hatchets, cruel silver blades flashing in the morning

light. There were so many that it looked like their own forest of death. In addition, they carried round wooden shields half the size of their bodies. Double protection for whatever was coming at them.

The men in the back of the lines, those without spears, unsheathed the long silver blades at their waists in a collective hiss. Then they beat the handle of those weapons against their shields and the quiet of the morning erupted into what sounded like rolling thunder. And then, in perfect unison, every soldier lifted his weapon in the air and gave a full-throated battle cry.

Kirra looked at the others in the tree. Everyone was glancing around with panic on their faces. Kirra made eye contact with each of her friends, slowly and deliberately thumping her heart with a fist. *Stay strong.*

Across the river, one of the soldiers shouted a command. In the front line, every tenth man stepped forward in unison, dropped his weapon, and lifted his hands in the air. The soldier behind him tied a long rope around his waist.

From the back of the ranks, large wooden posts were passed from soldier to soldier, and then handed to the roped men in the front.

Then these men marched into the river, carrying the posts overhead in two hands and trailing the rope behind them, while the other soldiers stayed put, holding on to the other end. As the water crept up to their waists and then their chests, the current threatened to knock them over and sweep them downstream. That's when Kirra realized what the ropes were for. The men on the opposite riverbank dug their heels into the sand and leaned back, keeping the men in the moving water anchored. In this manner, they were able to trudge forward, upright and secure, and emerge on her side of the river.

Once they were on the riverbank, the men put down their posts and removed shovels that were belted to their waists. After digging holes, they set the posts in the sand, packing them in tightly, working at a deliberate pace. Then each removed the rope from around his waist and tied it around the pole that was now sticking firmly upright in the ground.

And just like that, all the other soldiers had a swift and secure way to get across to the land of the Tree Folk.

The warriors strode into the rushing water one at a time at each rope, carrying their shields and weapons aloft, until so many of them covered the area that she could no longer see the riverbank itself. These trained soldiers were a mere stone's throw from the tree line and all the people who lived in the woods, all the people Kirra cared about.

They were close enough that Kirra could see their hard stares. These men had come with a purpose.

There were no speeches, no requests for negotiation or demands for surrender, no precursor at all. One man standing in front merely lifted his weapon in the air, pointed it straight at the forest, and screamed out a battle cry. Then he charged as fast as he could toward the trees, powerful legs churning beneath him.

The others followed by the hundreds, the earth shaking with the intensity of their approach.

26

TEEHA BLEW HER HORN ONCE and motioned to those in the trees in front of theirs, closer to the river.

Tree Folk hidden among the branches of four separate trunks leaped into action, jumping out of the limbs and assembling their puppet in an instant. Suddenly four forest giants appeared seemingly out of nowhere and stood in front of the advancing warriors. The people working the mouths screamed into their horns and pumped the levers that moved the jaws, and it looked like a quartet of monsters was bellowing and gnashing their teeth in rage.

The charge faltered as the soldiers took them in. These giants were enormous, at least twice again as large as the original one, and Kirra could tell by the wide eyes of the warriors that they were looking at more than they had bargained for.

But to the raiders' credit, their hesitation only lasted a moment before their battle cries increased in intensity and they resumed charging at double speed.

The two groups met in an explosion of violence. The giants smashed down with their great wooden fists, knocking soldiers this way and that, sweeping whole groups of them aside like dolls.

The giants stomped, too, their heavy log legs rising high in the air before crashing down on the warriors' helmets, knocking many of them senseless.

But there were just too many soldiers. They swarmed the giants from all sides, and soon the huge puppets were wading in a sea of them.

Several Takers jumped up as far as they could, grabbed the joints of the giants' knees and hung on fiercely, then climbed hand over hand toward the control center behind each giant's face. The people working the giants' arms had to spend their time and energy brushing these interlopers off their wooden bodies, and could no longer fight the ones on the ground.

This gave the warriors with hatchets the opening they

needed. Rushing right up to the giants, they began hacking away, the hefty blades digging in and sending showers of wood chips spraying into the air.

Soon the four towering giants were in bad shape. Three of them were missing arms where several invaders had climbed up the body, jumped onto the forearm, and hung there together, letting their combined weight rip the shoulder joint right out of the socket.

The giants were all stumbling around, their legs hacked up and decimated, threatening to give out altogether and come crashing down.

Teeha blew three short blasts on her horn: the signal for retreat.

The giants turned and limp-ran desperately for the trees like scared and wounded animals. They teetered unsteadily on chewed-up legs as they plunged through the underbrush. A roar of laughter erupted from the warriors below. *This was going to be too easy!* They regrouped into formation and marched resolutely after their prey, into the heart of the forest itself.

Kirra watched the Takers move directly underneath her tree, line after line of them, washing through like rolling waves.

When the four battered giants had plunged deep into the woods, the Tree Folk inside abandoned their sections, leaped into the branches of surrounding trees, and disappeared into the leaves. The giants clattered lifelessly to the ground, their parts reduced to debris on the forest floor.

The warriors stopped in their tracks, perplexed. There was no one left to charge. Standing in the middle of the trees, they looked down at the pieces of the giants, and then around at the still, silent forest. Had they won already?

That's when Teeha blew her horn again, one long and steady blast.

Attack.

Kirra and her crew leaped into action, and she traded her stationary spot in a solid tree for a perch in a walking giant.

All around, Tree Folk were doing the same. In a huge circle surrounding the soldiers, giants sprang to life everywhere. Ten, then twenty, thirty, and more. It was as if the entire forest were coming to life to protect this land.

That's when the real battle began.

Kirra lost perspective on the overall picture. Her world narrowed down to what was happening directly in front of her. Teeha's strong brothers were working the legs in unison, and her giant charged directly into the thick of the mass of warriors. Kirra held on tight with both hands as she was nearly jolted out of her seat, not expecting how violently the giant would stagger and shudder as it crashed against all of those solid, struggling bodies.

She and Luwan were working the same arm, and they swung it this way and that with all their might. The wood smashed against the enemy, snapping shields in half and sending bodies flying through the air.

"Look out!" Luwan yelled, and pointed behind her.

Kirra turned her head. From a crack between the sapling logs that made up the arm, she could see a raider climbing toward her. He had a knife clenched between his teeth and murderous rage in his eyes. As she knew from watching earlier, if enough of his fellow soldiers got up here, the giant's arm would be ripped off and she and Luwan would go tumbling into the roiling sea of soldiers with nothing to protect them. They would be stomped into oblivion, or pulled from the wreckage of the puppet to meet those cruel weapons.

Kirra grabbed one of a dozen sticks that she'd stashed near her perch for just this reason. The end of each stick had been sharpened to a point. She gripped it in both hands, waiting with bated breath until the warrior climbed right up to where she was seated, and then she jabbed the spike through a crack in the logs with all of her might.

The point caught the warrior in the face. He screamed and dropped to the forest floor. She turned and realized that Luwan was doing the same thing. Raising her head to look through a viewing portal, Kirra saw that their giant was free of climbing marauders for the moment.

She also got a broader look at the battle in the forest. It was impossible to tell which way it was going. True, the bodies of many soldiers were strewn about the forest floor.

But the giants had taken their losses as well. Some had limbs missing while others had been hacked apart entirely, the jagged pieces of their construction lying in ruins. The Tree Folk operating those giants had made the ultimate sacrifice for their land and their people. An overwhelming sadness threatened to paralyze Kirra, but she pushed that thought aside. They would honor their fallen brothers and sisters later. First there was still a job to be done.

"Teeha!" Makina screeched from the other side of the puppet, where she and Kharee were working the other arm. "Look! Over there! A group of them is trying to break the circle!"

Kirra knew this was bad. Their entire battle plan, after luring the Takers into the forest and ambushing them with the entire army of giants, was to corral the soldiers. Keep them contained, and fight them until they were all down or until they surrendered. If they let the circle be broken, the warriors could hide and regroup, and then the elements of surprise and control would be on *their* side. For the Tree Folk, unskilled in battle, this would spell doom. They had to finish this with the first wave of attacks or else they'd be at a serious disadvantage.

Teeha responded immediately. She thrust a brightly colored flag from the top of the giant's head, a signal to the surrounding giant puppets to follow her.

Her brothers worked the legs with everything they had,

and their giant raced toward the breach in the circle, where a mass of Takers had ripped down two puppets and were working on a third, making a hole in the line of defense that they could pour through.

Kirra's giant got there just in time with the reinforcements. They rushed into the hole, covering it like a leaky hole in the bottom of a gourd.

Three soldiers managed to slip through before the reinforcements got there. Teeha directed her brothers and the giant chased them down. Luwan and Kirra worked the arms in a frenzy of activity. Together, they thrust an enormous wooden hand down at the warriors, scooped them all up in a single handful, and then smashed them against the broad trunk of a nearby tree. The warriors fell numbly to the ground.

Their giant worked with the others to repel the invaders trying to bust through. The soldiers finally gave up, turned, and ran to help in another part of the battle, but it was becoming increasingly difficult for the enemy to find a strategic place to join the fight. Although some of the giants were maimed or had been brought down altogether, most of the army still stood.

Kirra's heart soared at the sight. They were winning! They were going to do this!

"Oh no." Luwan barely croaked it out, but Kirra was able to hear him since they were so close together. "Oh no."

She turned to look at him and found an expression on his face of utter shock and dismay.

"What?" she screamed at him. "What is it?"

He merely pointed into the distance. Her gaze followed.

And there, back toward the river, she saw the one thing that frightened a forest dweller more than anything else in this world.

Smoke.

27

"TEEHA!" LUWAN SHOUTED. "Look! We have to go to the river!"

The master builder shook her head emphatically. "We will stick to the plan."

"But the Takers have plans of their own! So that means that ours has to change. We have to adapt!"

Teeha just looked straight ahead grimly and continued to shout orders to the rest of the crew, keeping a firm line at the perimeter of the battle and crushing any raiders who tried to break through.

The clouds of smoke grew darker, billowed up thicker from the direction of the river.

Luwan turned to face Kirra. "I respect Teeha, but she can be stubborn. Good luck." He started to work his way out of the seat.

"But what are you going to—"

"I have to help. Wish me luck!"

And with that he wormed his way through the branches that made up the arm, took a running leap into the limbs of a nearby tree, and disappeared.

Kirra's heart raced as she continued to work the arm of the giant alone. She never imagined having to fight without Luwan, and the prospect of doing so now was deeply disturbing. As were the increasingly thick clouds of smoke that were creeping into the forest itself, spreading through the battle and the branches. She could smell them.

A high-pitched horn sounded a series of staccato blasts. The signal for distress, to be used in dire emergencies only. It came from somewhere near the river.

"We have to get over there!" Kirra shouted.

Teeha nodded. Responding to the horn was part of the agreed-upon plan. She shouted down to her brothers, and the giant lurched into action, heading back to where it had come from.

Kirra surveyed the scene as they lumbered through the woods. It seemed like they had won—many of the giants were still in working condition and most of the warriors seemed unable to continue fighting, incapacitated in one way or another.

So what could be happening with that distress call? And why was the smoke getting worse?

She saw for herself when their giant burst through the tree line and out onto the wide riverbank.

A huge bonfire was roaring there, on the Tree Folk's side. It was circled by warriors, who were dipping long sticks with material wrapped around the ends into the fire. The tips ignited in an instant, blooming with crackling red flames. The soldiers passed the torches down the line. They were going to burn them out!

Standing in front of the fire, leading this terrible assault, was Red Streak. He waved a torch over his head with an impossibly long gray arm, tracing a ring of fire in the sky as he bellowed at the top of his lungs, exhorting his troops.

The warriors with torches attacked the advancing giant puppets, swarming them and lighting them up in several places.

The giants spun around. If they ran back into the safety of the forest, they would bring the flames with them and burn their homeland to the ground. If they stayed and fought, they would be incinerated.

So they ran for the river and dove in, surrendering them-selves to the water. Hissing steam rose from the current. Red

Streak threw back his head and roared with laughter as he watched his enemies rendered useless.

The rest of the giants were paralyzed, caught between forest and river.

"Should we retreat?" Teeha shouted at Kirra over the noise of the battle. "Form another circle in the woods?"

Kirra shook her head. "They will follow and burn us all down."

"But they will ruin the forest! They will have gained nothing!"

Kirra saw the crazed look on Red Streak's face, the wild eyes as he laughed and screamed at his men. "They don't care," she yelled back. "If they can't have victory, they will settle for destruction."

A wave of overwhelming despair crashed over Kirra. Not obliteration by fire. Not again.

But what to do? Red Streak's plan was turning the puppets into nothing more than kindling. And they couldn't fight on the ground, hand to hand with the warriors and their vicious weapons. It would be a bloodbath.

What to do? Oh, dear gods, what could they do?

That's when Makina screamed, "Look!" and pointed to the sky.

Here came Luwan, curved poles in each hand, streaming down from the upper branches. Falling as fast as a stone, he was a hawk with fury in his eyes.

He was followed by Hook Hunters, dozens and dozens of them. They silently dropped out of the trees, from everywhere. It was a summer storm, a rainy season of pure vengeance.

To Kirra's mind, what took place next looked as if the torch-wielding warriors were a group of boars and the Hook Hunters hadn't had a decent meal in a month.

Each soldier carrying fire was the target of a missile from the sky. The Hook Hunters rained down on them, clubbing the invaders senseless and stamping on the torches until the flames went out.

Other soldiers rushed to the bonfire, perhaps trying to get enough torches ready to overwhelm their adversaries. But two quick-thinking giant teams came walking up, holding between them the upside-down roof of one of the Tree Folk huts. They had dipped it into the river, and it was spilling over with water.

The warriors turned in time to see them arrive, but it was too late to react. The giants, working in unison, dumped their makeshift bucket on the bonfire, extinguishing the flames with a great hiss.

As steam from the dying embers rose to the sky, the steam seemed to seep out of what was left of the Taker army. The remaining warriors looked at the forest, where they'd been soundly beaten, and at the dead fire, which had clearly been their only hope of pulling off a victory.

One warrior turned and ran for the river, and he was quickly joined by others. In a matter of moments, the current was churning with soldiers clinging to the ropes that had been set up, straining to get to the opposite shore. When the first warriors to retreat hit the tree line on the other side, they disappeared into the brush and kept on running.

Red Streak screamed at the men—he clearly wanted them to stay and keep fighting, even if it meant the sacrifice of every man's life. But the rest of the Takers were not listening. They'd had enough.

Kirra leaned over and gave Teeha instructions. The normally stoic builder broke into a huge grin. "You got it."

Their giant stalked over to Red Streak. The burly warrior grabbed a huge hatchet and set his feet shoulder width apart, ready for one last fight.

Kirra worked the giant's arm so it swept down and scooped up Red Streak in its fist. The man bellowed in rage.

Kharee and Makina abandoned their arm and scrambled over to her side. They pulled on the ropes until the arm bent at the elbow and brought Red Streak back, inch by struggling inch. Makina lashed the rope tightly, holding the arm in place.

Red Streak, caught upside down in the branches and unable to claw his way out, shouted and spluttered. But when the giant's arm was fully pulled back into firing position,

Kirra removed a few of the branches that made up the arm's construction and came face-to-face with him.

"This is for Zedu," she said. Kirra slammed her cutting stone down on the rope that Makina had cinched up, and it snapped cleanly in two.

The catapult arm shot forward, sending Red Streak screaming through the sky, sailing over fifty feet high in the air, before crashing down into the river.

They had made sure to throw him past the safety lines. The current swept him down the river and out of sight forever.

28

KIRRA HAD COME TO THE LAKE EARLY, seeking a quiet place to think. And for a while, she had it all to herself, the soft morning sunlight filtering through the leaves and shimmering on the surface of the water.

But a curious thing happened while she sat there on the grass of the little meadow. People started to filter into the clearing from the trees. And not just a few of them, but many, many Tree Folk came out into the open to enjoy this beautiful morning.

They gave Kirra her space, but they offered her warm

smiles and friendly waves as they walked by, greeting her by name. Before the events of the last few months, only a handful of people ever acknowledged her presence. Now it seemed that everyone in the forest knew her name.

And she wasn't the only one who had made new connections. As she observed her surroundings, she saw that people were not clustered in little groups of two or three anymore. Big gatherings were forming. Three and four and five families coming together to share food and splash in the water, the adults talking among themselves while the children ran wild, laughing and playing.

Again, Kirra felt like she could have been back in Zedu. She smiled wistfully—would that make what she was about to do easier, or more difficult?

"You look like you have something on your mind, meerkat."

She turned to see Mome walking up behind her.

"May I sit with you for a spell?"

She patted the grass next to her. "Of course."

He settled in beside her but didn't say anything. Mome could do silence better than anyone she had ever met.

Finally, she gestured all around, at everyone who was filling up the meadow and the lake. "Did someone invite all these people down here today? For a celebration, or something?"

"Of course." He gave her a sidelong look and raised one eyebrow. "You did."

She wrinkled her brow. "Um, no. I didn't. I would've remembered that."

Mome grinned. "Perhaps you didn't make an announcement. But you have shown them a different way. They have an open invitation to gather, and they are enjoying it. I would venture to say there will be many such celebrations from now on, all over the forest."

Kirra watched a gaggle of small children chase one another around on the shore, while others stood in the lake, trying to splash them. They were all shrieking with delight. "It makes me happy to see them happy."

They were silent for a while again. Finally, Mome gestured to the knapsacks lying at her feet. "Are you traveling somewhere?"

She took a deep breath, admitting it to herself as much as to him. "I am."

"Ah. I thought so."

"Are you . . . I don't know, mad at me?"

He placed a scarred hand over hers. "I'll be sad to see you go, because I will miss you. But I have said good-bye to many good friends in many places. I understand the need to leave when you feel the time is right."

"Do you feel the time is right?"

"For you to leave? Only one person in this world can answer that." He gazed at her with his kind eyes. "Have you told your family?"

She sighed. "Yes. Last night."

"How did they take it?"

She chewed on her lip. "Not very well, at first. Especially Luwan. They have always been here, so it's harder for them to imagine anyplace else."

He nodded.

"Loba blames you. At least partially."

Mome raised his eyebrows. "And why is that?"

"On the ridge, after I gave my big speech and you stood up for me . . . And when you told me that what happened before, in Zedu, wasn't my fault . . . That's when I first started to think about leaving."

Mome nodded again. "I understand. I didn't want you to feel you had to carry that burden of shame any longer. It was too heavy, and it wasn't your burden anyway. Similarly, you must not carry the burden of having saved us. Everyone played a part."

"Oh, I know!" Kirra said quickly, eager to show her agreement. "We all did it together."

She didn't think she would ever forget the collective feeling of elation she and the Tree Folk had experienced immediately after their victory. Wild cheering and dancing had broken out, Teeha had been lifted onto people's shoulders, and Luwan—well, Loba hadn't batted an eye when his son declared his intention to be a Hook Hunter.

The joy had soon been tempered by the reality of the

losses they had suffered. They'd spent days burying and mourning their dead, and weeks cleaning up the river and forest.

The recovery process was ongoing. It would be slow, but beautiful days like this one helped heal the community. And Kirra could plainly see that it was much more of a community than ever before.

Mome brought her out of her thoughts. "The only thing you should carry is the truth, which you have done admirably." He looked up at the sky, then back at her. "And now I'm guessing that you'd like to carry it farther?"

"I am a Storyteller." Her voice was clear, all traces of hesitation or doubt gone. "Like my father. My *first* father. And Storytellers travel."

"Will you tell people about the Takers?"

"That's part of it, yes. But there are lots of stories to tell. Some I learned from my father, some from you, but most I have picked up from my own experiences, everything that I've seen."

Mome shook his head slowly. "You've been through so much . . . It seems you have packed several lifetimes into your few years already." He put an arm around her and pulled her close for a hug. "It would be quite remarkable to see what you do with the rest of your years."

She grinned and leaned into him. "Well, maybe you will. Luwan's family made me promise to come back at the start of every dry season. I have to stay at least a month, and they promise to fatten me up and listen to my new stories."

"They are good people."

"So are you."

Mome patted her shoulder and then stood up and stretched, his old back cracking and popping. "Well, I should probably get going. As you say, there's much to see and much to be done."

"Any other words of advice?"

He thought again, weighing her words. "You have a gift. I'm glad you've chosen to share it with the world."

She smiled, trying to keep her tears at bay. "I'll see you again in the dry season."

Mome walked away for a few steps, paused in midstride, and then doubled back. "There is one more thing. . . . I wasn't sure whether or not I would tell you, because I hear many things and not all of them turn out to be true."

"Yes . . . ?"

He searched the clearing with his eyes, and then they settled back on her. "I have heard of a man who has been walking from village to village across the great lands over the last few seasons. He is a master Storyteller, and he wins every competition he enters."

Kirra sat up straighter.

Mome added, "He has also been warning people about the Takers."

Kirra couldn't breathe, just stared at him for several moments. "Paja?" she whispered. Was there a chance he could have escaped from the volcano?

Mome merely shrugged. "I do not know, meerkat. As I say, I hear many tales, and truth can be a slippery thing. But it's something to keep in mind for your travels." He bent over and gently kissed the top of her head; then he turned and was gone.

Kirra's belly was full of butterflies and her mind was going in a hundred directions. But she had become good at juggling several different ideas and emotions at the same time. She took a deep breath before she too stood, stretched, and picked up her pouches.

She walked to the edge of the clearing, taking a moment to soak in the spirit of kinship that was radiating from all these people enjoying the day together.

Then she turned back and walked toward the trail out of the forest.

She did not know if it was part of her story to ever see her father again. But in any case, she intended to live a life that would make him proud.

Authors' Notes

THIS STORY BEGAN TO TAKE SHAPE while I was living in New Orleans. I found inspiration in the branches of the beautiful live oaks that lined the streets and filled the parks.

I have always loved being in the woods. As a kid I spent days climbing trees and playing in the forests around my home in New York State. I pretended I'd find secret communities of people never before seen by the outside world. I used to feel like the forest was watching me.

Because of my parents, I grew up in different parts of the world—primarily in North America and Southern Africa. I think my love of nature came from all the time we spent enjoying the unspoiled wilderness and the hospitality of the people who lived there.

I admire communities that manage to live in balance with nature. There are infinite lessons to be learned from these people.

I marvel at other communities that can be found in wilderness, too. The complexities that have evolved are astounding. The bivouac or army ants are a good example of a seemingly impossible adaptation for survival. The entire community—the queen, the eggs, the workers, and the soldiers—all live in a colony made entirely out of their own living bodies. By linking their legs, they create a huge fortress to protect their population from harm. At a moment's notice they can unlock their legs and move on.

I imagined what it would be like if humans were able to be like those army ants. What if the small people of my childhood dreams could link arms and become bigger and stronger and safer?

It was in New Orleans that I began to think up the characters in this story and how they might triumph over adversity by working together.

I told the story to my children. I told it to my friends. They all told me to write it down, my tale of the little people who became giants. The more people I told, the more I felt my story was worth telling.

That's where Clete came in. He made my vision come alive with convincing and distinctive characters. Out of my twigs and leaves he constructed a fully realized world in which people can live in dormant volcanoes, or villages, or giant trees. He patiently listened to my ramblings and turned them into a project I am grateful to be a part of and proud to share with you. He is a beautiful storyteller. This book would simply never have been written were it not for him.

I hope it inspires you to dream, too.

—Dave Matthews

WHEN I WAS A KID, I would hike through the forests of the Pacific Northwest and make up fantastical stories. The most recurring idea from those walks was that there was an entire society hidden in the upper boughs of the trees. I was fascinated by the possibility. How did the community get there, and why? What did the inhabitants look like? How did their secret village operate? I spent hours scanning the treetops, trying to catch a glimpse of them.

I never wrote that story, but I happened to mention the idea one day when I was having lunch with my wonderful editor, Stephanie Lurie. Imagine the thrill when she called me years later and invited me to collaborate with a storyteller who had a project that included part of this premise. Imagine my further thrill when that person turned out to be Dave Matthews. Finally I would get to dive into this idea that had long fascinated me. And then, over dinner with Dave, I learned that his vision also included an epic tale about love and loss, betrayal and redemption, and what it means to live in true community with others—including all the accompanying struggles and joys. It felt like not only a fun story but also an important one. I was all in.

Dave was collaborative and creative and kind on every step of this journey. I remain awed by his passion for imaginative projects. So many people around the world have enjoyed the creativity he has to offer; I'm excited for them to get to experience his story and so grateful to have been a part of it.

—Clete Smith